ated markdown
# The Obsidian Villain

Vasilisa Drake

Copyright © 2024 by Vasilisa Drake

All rights reserved.

No portion of this book may be reproduced in any form without written permission from the publisher or author, except as permitted by U.S. copyright law.

# Contents

| | |
|---|---|
| Dedication | 1 |
| Chapter 1 | 2 |
| Chapter 2 | 13 |
| Chapter 3 | 19 |
| Chapter 4 | 25 |
| Chapter 5 | 37 |
| Chapter 6 | 47 |
| Chapter 7 | 54 |
| Chapter 8 | 66 |
| Chapter 9 | 71 |
| Chapter 10 | 82 |
| Chapter 11 | 88 |
| Chapter 12 | 94 |
| Chapter 13 | 100 |
| Chapter 14 | 107 |

| | |
|---|---|
| Chapter 15 | 113 |
| Chapter 16 | 118 |
| Epilogue | 122 |
| Bonus Chapter | 126 |
| Acknowledgments | 134 |
| About the Author | 137 |
| Find Vasilisa | 140 |

*To Tinder, for making me realize I'd rather have a dragon kidnap me than go on another first date.*

# Chapter 1

LENORA TASHE HAD NEVER before regretted not having tumbled in the sheets, half-drunk after a harvest celebration with some farmer's son.

Not until it meant that the village decided her intact maidenhood made her a perfect sacrifice for the dragon tyrant.

"Come on, Nora, don't be mad at them," one of said farmer's sons whined from the horse trotting beside her. "You know they didn't have a choice."

Nora kept her gaze straight ahead. Her hands were bound to stop her from fleeing. It was obvious she was the victim of this arrangement, and she was under no obligation to absolve Garth of his guilt.

"Do you really want to go there mad?" he continued, his nasal voice grating on her.

"'Go there'?" Nora repeated before she could stop herself, her temper fraying. "By there, perchance you mean into the maw of that great beast?"

"Someone had to," Garth protested. No doubt the boy was unused to people being angry with him. He passed for good looking in their village, with long blonde curls and blue eyes that twinkled when he tried to flirt, skin that was tan from honest labor, but not so tan that you couldn't see the blush on his cheeks. He did, however, possess the last attractive quality a man could have in Nora's view: he had no problem selling her off to a dragon.

"Someone? It could've been some sheep the way it had been the past fifty years!"

Every year the dragon demanded his due: clothing, livestock, precious jewels, piles of gold. The village of Mossley had nothing more to offer than a paltry amount of animals each year, but even that offering was almost prohibitively expensive. A dragon might devour a dozen animals in one sitting, if the rumors were true. But that same livestock kept the village alive through hard seasons.

The life of one girl? Well, it was worth less than the half-dozen sheep she took the place of.

"You know what Bess said. It had to be someone *pure*, someone to appease the beast. You're our best hope, Nora. You should be proud to serve the village this way."

If she heard the word pure again, she might very well use her bound hands to lean over and strangle the man escorting her. She had considered it more than once on their journey.

But the truth of the matter was, even if she left, she had nowhere to go. She had lived in Mossley her whole life, and they had voted to send her off based on the ramblings of a madwoman.

Her own stepmother had been the first to put her up, boasting Nora's untouched maidenhood. Who knew having more of an interest in books than village boys would be a death sentence?

Because that is what it was. No matter what Crazy Bess had claimed, the dragon would eat her. Beasts did not wed, not as humans did.

*He seeks a maiden, pure and blessed. No simple mutton will satisfy his carnal needs. If we give him this, a bride, we will finally be spared this tragedy. I have seen it!* The old woman had raved for weeks leading up to the tithe.

Never mind the strange words she'd said in parting, whispered only to Nora.

"Of course, this is the time everyone decides to listen to her," she muttered under her breath.

"Hmm?" Garth had been distracted as he turned his attention to the map. Because the boy needed a map to make the half day's journey to the meeting spot.

Nora was silent the rest of the ride.

They reached the meeting point and were among the last to arrive.

Woe be to any who attempted to skip out. The sun would be blocked out by a span of wings, and whatever unlucky villagers would find themselves without homes when the dragon was through.

And any who dared be miserly with their offering?

The dirt was littered with scorch marks as evidence of past years' dissatisfaction.

Mossley was one of the smaller villages in the area. Other towns offered as they usually did—sheep, cattle, any manner of livestock would do, though word was the dragon was not overly fond of poultry. But this was the meeting spot for everyone who was tithing, including the highest powers in the land. On the other side could be none other than His Majesty's representative. Nora tried to make out what they had brought this year.

An ornately carved golden chaise with jewels embedded on the edges. Any one of those jewels could buy her entire village.

She supposed she should be flattered.

A figure emerged from behind the metal couch. He was dressed more finely than any of the others and rode his horse with an air of presumption that was foreign to everyone in her village except perhaps her stepmother when she had a choice bit of gossip. It was the stance of someone with a measure of power.

"People of Wyrdova! We thank you for your sacrifices this year. The great obsidian beast will arrive shortly. Do not fear, for the demon will delight in it! Know you are safe, so long as your offering is suitably impressive." The Prince of Wyrdova not-so-subtly indicated the heap of precious metal next to him.

His eyes snagged on Nora. There was nothing remarkable about Nora's flaxen hair or the simple smock she wore. Nothing that should warrant a prince's interest.

He trotted over to Garth and Nora all the same. "Tell me, villagers, where do you hail from and what bounty do you offer? Tell me you did not forget." This was directed to Garth more than Nora. For one, she was a woman, and not an authority on anything so complex as where she hailed from, in the eyes of the prince. And secondly, her hands were bound, marking her as the tithe rather than another representative.

"Uh, Your Highness." Garth dipped his head in acknowledgment, then bobbed again, as if doing an impression of a clucking hen. "We are from Mossley. And, well, our seer suggested our suffering may end if we offer up a maiden, pure and chaste."

It took a valiant effort to not roll her eyes. Though it hardly mattered, since she would likely be dead by sunset.

Instead, she helpfully lifted her bound wrists to show it was hardly *voluntary* madness.

The prince opened his mouth to protest, but his words were drowned out by the thunderous sound of ocean waves.

No. Nora would have smacked herself if her hands were free. It was not the ocean that roared around them. The rush of wind that blew through the field was as powerful as any spring storm. Her hair was tucked in plaits across her crown, the only thing that stopped it from whipping around her the way the prince's golden locks now did.

It had been bright, not a cloud in the sky, with still a smattering of hours until sundown, yet the sun was suddenly blotted out by a massive figure.

The effect was terrifying.

The dragon slammed down to the ground in the center, fifty horse-lengths away.

It was an effort not to quake atop her own, which whinnied in fear.

She'd grown up with tales of the obsidian dragon who extorted Wyrdova. It was the horror story told to keep little children in line; it was the terror told over a few pints of ales in an increasingly dramatic fashion.

But none compared to the sight before her.

Wings as wide as several houses spread as the beast landed, first rearing on its hind legs before stomping forward. They reflected the light with blistering intensity. Gazing at the beast was painful until it folded its massive wingspan against itself. But the retraction made the beast no less terrifying; instead, it highlighted the rest of its features. Black scales rippled across its skin, with long fangs fitting over its maw as it faced them.

Nora's heart nearly stopped as it fixed its gray, reptilian eyes on her.

*It's just examining its haul*, she assured herself.

On silent cue, people began to present their offerings to the dragon. The prince had moved back, grandly presenting the golden chaise—from a safe distance, twenty paces behind the servants, His Highness had ordered it carried forward.

The pile in front of the dragon grew and grew: a crowd of livestock, more gold bars from the wealthier territories, books that Nora would never have been able to find in her small village, textiles even the mayor would not have been able to afford in a lifetime.

And then Nora was pushed forward on the pile.

Just Nora. Garth aided—forced—her to dismount from her steed. The village was not willing to lose a horse in this exchange.

Where all the rest had been able to keep a distance from the dragon, Nora was now a mere dozen steps away from it, amidst a mass of sheep and cows.

One eye seemed to follow her to her position.

*Be brave, Nora. For once in your life, be brave.* She would not cower as she faced her death.

Even when its maw suddenly snapped forward, devouring in one solid bite several animals that had been next to her, she forced herself to stand, locking her knees in determination.

But when it suddenly rose and grabbed Nora with a three-pointed claw, she screamed. Her heart pounded in her throat, choking her as it became impossible to breathe.

The dragon was airborne with a flap of its wings. Higher and higher they went. Garth and the horses grew smaller until they were specks, and then they were nothing as the dragon flew away from the villages and towards the mountain range.

Her screaming stopped as she gasped for breath and looked below her. It was the most terrifying, exhilarating thing Nora had ever done.

The sun began to set, and if not for the fact she was near being sick, she would've marveled at the colors at this close distance.

But the sunset was not long as the mountains drew closer and closer. Even in her distant village, she knew this was where the dragons made their nests. Kept their troves.

The dragon flew into a cave that seemingly appeared from nowhere. Nora was unceremoniously dropped onto the cave floor, along with whatever the dragon had pulled from the tithe. Books; textiles; the garish chaise. It had not been able to take everything, but the dragon was known to return at its leisure for the offerings. Save on one day each year, all knew to steer clear of the field where the taxes were left.

One did not steal from a dragon.

It landed, its tail swaying about as it rounded back to face Nora and inspect its haul.

Nora barely breathed. Only stared.

And stared.

And stared.

The dragon regarded her with a blink and then began to flip through the piles with one massive claw as if the beast could read and consider.

Finally, she could take it no longer.

"Well?" she demanded. "Are you going to eat me?"

The dragon huffed out some smoke, what might have been amusement, and settled down on the ground, resting its massive head on crossed forelegs. Massive, scaled eyelids settled shut over those unnervingly intelligent reptilian eyes as if the beast now desired a nap.

It was an odd thing, to be so ready to die and then to be dismissed. It wasn't relief that flooded Nora.

It was rage.

Rage that this creature had tormented her people for years. That it bled them dry of their meager wealth. That it had cost Nora her own home. Made the people she'd known her entire life willing to cast her out on a mad woman's words.

A mad woman who had whispered more to Nora on the way out. Words she'd discarded because she'd expected her death to be swift.

Death would come. Nora didn't doubt that. But it need not be hers.

*When you wed the beast, you may save us all, girl,* Crazy Bess had said. *A dragon never lowers its guard save when it retreats to its trove and sheds its scales. Only pieces of its own self can pierce the beast's heart. You must get close when it least expects it, and when you defeat the beast, we will all be safe.*

So that was what Nora would do.

She would kill the dragon.

## Chapter 2

THE MAIDEN WAS NEW. He had been offered any number of trinkets over the years, but this was the first time the humans had decided to part with one of their own.

He hadn't yet decided if he was insulted or flattered.

Upon seeing her, even before she'd been led over to him, he'd decided he would have her. Dragons enjoyed acquiring all manner of lovely things, and indeed, she was counted among that number.

Most humans looked alike. But there was something about her. The way she sat atop the horse, proud and angry. Her unflinching gaze—well... unflinching, until he'd finally picked her up and hauled her to his trove. If the screaming had lasted much longer, he might have dropped her just to spare his ears.

He regarded her now with curiosity, through the barest slits of his eyes. He wanted to know what she would do.

Escape, no doubt. Oh, she wouldn't get far, but it might be entertaining to watch her try.

Alistair was in desperate need of entertainment.

Life had gotten dull. Even his yearly haul from this kingdom—he of course harvested from all the local kingdoms, one kingdom each season—did not cheer him. How his only kin had gone to other lands centuries ago and not been seen since. Maybe he needed more treasure. One could never have too much gold.

But perhaps there was another issue.

He went unchallenged. Everyone was afraid of him.

Well, with good reason. Word of his wicked deeds kept the puny mortals in line. He could stomach the indigestion the suits of iron gave him as he swallowed some of the king's men, as a reminder that he was not a dragon to be messed with, but having a fearsome reputation cut down on the stomach aches required.

Oh, they had tried to kill him in the beginning. If he had been a lesser dragon, perhaps an amethyst or peridot one, one of their attempts might have even been successful.

But Alistair was an obsidian dragon.

There was but one thing that could kill him, and some over-confident soldier seeking his fortune was not it.

Boredom was a disease. After the past few years, it had taken root in him, a restlessness under his skin that unsettled him that he could not escape, not even when he flew high above the clouds.

He considered the female.

To his surprise, she had not yet attempted to flee.

No, she kept glancing at him, to see if he stirred, but he'd had centuries to hone his skills, and deceiving a simple human was nothing at all.

He resisted the urge to snore dramatically to set her at ease that he was "truly" asleep. His snores were known to shake mountains and might startle the tiny female.

Instead of attempting to scamper off, she examined his haul. Her fingers lingered on one of the tomes the scribes had offered him. She lifted the jeweled cover and began to page through the book.

Usually, Alistair despised others touching his hoard.

He had set others, including—*especially*—other dragons on fire for less.

There was something different about this human. He had begun to suspect he knew the reason, but he could not be certain. Not in this form.

Perhaps it was simply that she was part of his hoard. It made sense. He did not get jealous over his books when a piece of textile draped over them. Why should he mind her?

She was simply a belonging.

Unless...

She turned from the books and examined the rest of the haul. He hadn't brought everything. The livestock was cumbersome; animals had a habit of defecating in his claws when he carried them, but at least they were tasty. He would return when he wanted an easy snack. Normally, he made a few trips to carry everything, but for some reason, he did not want to leave this female's company.

Was she impressed by the wealth he had inspired the others to part with? Alistair never let others see his hoard, so he had no one to show off to. Not that he *needed* the validation. But surely it was more wealth than the female had ever dreamed of.

She *should* be impressed.

But she barely contained a scoff as she took in the golden chaise he'd been offered and thumbed through the textiles with hardly a care.

She was dressed in the manner of peasants, or at least, that was what Alistair assumed. He didn't spend much time studying the breed. One, they were inferior. Two, they tended to run away screaming, and it had gotten bothersome to try.

Humans also tended to defecate in his claws on the rare occasion he deigned to carry them. It was a mark in the female's favor that she had not done so.

Would she take some of the fine fabrics and change? He would allow it; she was part of his hoard after all. It reflected badly on him to have a female in such shambles. Even through the tiniest slits of his eyelids, it was obvious her clothing was old and frayed. Holes in her smock; worn boots on her feet. At least she had bathed recently. Sometimes humans forgot, and he was tempted to incinerate the smelly ones on principle.

But she ignored the textiles.

Alistair bit back on the urge to huff. What, it wasn't good enough for her?

But she seemed to be on a mission. Instead of moving towards the exit, she moved farther into the caves. His hoard was buried deep in the mountain, as was proper, but he had a few fragments around, piles of old offerings that decorated the space.

She appeared to be searching for something.

But what could it be?

He twisted his head to see as she moved out of his sight. She flinched at the noise, and he quickly settled back down. A palm was pressed against her generous bosom as if steadying herself.

Alistair bit down a laugh, or what passed for a laugh in this form. The urge startled him. When was the last time he'd had such an impulse?

This human... he would keep her for a while, he decided. She would not solve the permanent issue of boredom that plagued him, but she could be his entertainment for a time.

She continued farther, past where he could see. He had a choice: reveal his human form to her now and set his expectations straight, or wait. Wait and see what mischief his human got up to.

She continued to quietly step deeper into the cave.

He could be patient, he decided. She would be around for so little time, in the grand duration of his life, that he could afford to draw this out with her. He could *savor*.

So he stayed exactly where he was.

Waiting.

Waiting.

Until she screamed, the sound echoing off the maze of caves and coating them in terror.

# Chapter 3

Nora screamed.

She hadn't meant to. She clapped her hands over her mouth, even as she pressed her back against the cave wall, as far away from that... that *creature* as she could manage.

It blinked back at her with wide, curious eyes. Eyes that were far too wide. It was unlike anything Nora had ever seen before. Unlike anything she'd read about.

Its body was like a cat, but malformed, with large ears that twitched as it examined her, and horns that curved backward. Its legs were muscled with patchy fur like a goat's until its feet tapered off into chicken claws. Similarly, short, uneven chicken wings came from the side, the features an utter mess.

And it glowed. A pale burnt orange shone directly from its skin.

It was as tall as her chest when it sat on its haunches. The creature tilted its head in question, still blinking, as if to ask, *Who are you?*

Nora didn't move from her spot, still cursing herself for screaming.

*Stupid Nora, now you've woken the beast. The dragon will decide to eat you if this creature doesn't kill you first, before you even had a chance to find one of its scales!*

Because that, she'd deciphered, was what Mad Bess had meant. Not the bride part—that was nonsense, since she could hardly wed a dragon. In the trove, the dragon would shed its scales, and only those scales would be strong enough to pierce its armored chest.

Not that it mattered. The creature lifted from its haunches and stepped toward her, sniffing loudly.

She was frozen in her spot, unable to flee.

Closer it came, its eyes focused, like those of a predator. It looked the same way her old barn cat had when the lazy thing finally spotted a lame mouse.

She very nearly screamed when a voice said, "So, you've met Morthil."

Nora spun, taking her gaze away from the creature to face the voice against her better instincts.

And then she shrieked again.

In front of her was a man.

A man... and that was all. He stood in all his glory, the lights on the wall of the cave illuminating every perfectly carved inch of him. And between his legs...

She knew the way animals mated. Logically, she knew if she went for a roll in the hay—or marital bed—it would bear some similarities.

But... *that*.

That would not *fit*.

Just the thought made her feel faint. And worse, she felt some stirring that was wholly inappropriate for a young maiden to feel after being sacrificed to a dragon.

Her gaze slammed upward.

He was the most beautiful man she had ever laid eyes on. His beauty was otherworldly. Dark locks fell to his shoulder, glistening like glass. His face was fitted in panes, a sharp jaw, deep cheeks, an angular neck.

But the eyes... the eyes were not human. They were gray, slit like a reptile.

Just as the dragon's had been.

Now, he cocked his head, pressing a palm to one ear. Even in this shape, his black claws remained, the nails the same color as they'd been on the dragon and shaped like talons. "Must you scream? I thought something might be wrong."

"You're... you're..."

"Alistair Obsidian-Claw," he replied with a dramatic bow, before lifting his head in a cheeky grin. His voice was smooth as unbroken water, rinsing over her like a calming balm.

"You're the dragon!"

"The dragon," he pondered. "Well, I am *a* dragon. The dragon that now owns you."

His lips tipped up in a way that sent shivers down Nora's spine, his words laced with a possessiveness that scared her. She tried to back farther away, but she only hit the hard stone of the cave.

With her attention fixed on the man—dragon—*Alistair*, she had lost sight of the godforsaken creature and jolted when it pressed against her.

But instead of opening its maw and eating her, the creature just stayed there, leaning into her.

"He's taken a liking to you," Alistair said, as if it was a good thing.

Nora lifted her hands, trying to keep far away from Morthil, who seemed determined to maintain contact with her. "What *is* he?"

"Morthil's rather lonely, especially as you refuse to pet him." The dejected tone was so overdone it barely covered Alistair's obvious amusement.

"Must you twist my words?" Nora snapped.

Then she shrank farther against the wall. What was she doing, speaking back to a dragon? Did she *want* to die?

No. She wanted to kill the beast and return to her town a hero, finally welcomed as a full member of society.

But she didn't want to do that with her tail between her legs.

Alistair laughed. The sound was almost rusty, like his jaw was unused to moving in such a way. "There is much I take pleasure in, female, that I do not have to do. I'm not one to deny myself."

Morthil made a sound at her feet, drawing her attention.

Finally, in desperation, she lowered a hand and pet the top of the swallump's head. It was not so different from the barn cat she'd grown up with. Aside from the fact it was ten times the size.

The creature made a sound that, if she was half-deaf, could have been construed as a purr.

"There. Fast friends, my pets are."

Her head swung once more to the dragon. He had come closer, on silent feet, and now stood a few feet away.

The good news was the organ between his legs was out of view.

The bad news was, there was no escaping those reptilian eyes. Nora suspected they must be magic, because once they captured her, she could not look away.

"I am *not* your pet."

"You are mine." There was an edge to the smooth words, a blade that dared her to argue. "Your own people gave you away. Be angry with them, not me."

She *had* been angry with them. But it was hard to be angry with the only family, the only community she had ever known. It was desperation that made them trade her off, she decided. She would win them back once the dragon was defeated, and they were safe.

But Alistair, who dared look at her like she belonged to him? Like he owned her, from her body to the very thoughts she wrapped around her soul?

Oh, him she could be angry with.

Him, she could *hate*.

# Chapter 4

OH, THE HUMAN FEMALE was shaping up to be *quite* a lot of fun.

First, he had found her pressed against the wall, terrified of the baby swallump Alistair had adopted a decade ago. The thing was just curious about a potential new playmate, and she had screamed in terror.

She hadn't even looked that afraid of him! It was all he could do not to double over in laughter.

Then there was the indignant way she challenged him. He had not conversed with a human in some time, but by memory, they were not so prickly! They were scared of him and fled, or on occasion bored him with a righteous speech.

They didn't banter with him. Their words didn't attempt to singe him, as though their tongues could produce fire.

Yet his human did. This pleased him.

Her form pleased him, too. It was different to see her in the eyes of his human shape. Better, even. The locks glittered like his hoard of gold in the torchlight. The perfect bow of her lips that beckoned him until it opened to attack. Her eyes, pale as ice, widened with fear and shrank with fury with such speed he couldn't help but relish in. She was small, even when he compared her to his stature in this form instead of a massive dragon. At most, she reached his shoulder, and that was generous as she was in boots. The comely shape of her hips, buried beneath layers of fabric. The large chest covered by that rag she called a frock.

He wanted to get rid of it. Either to cover her with something finer, more suitable for his female, or simply destroy it entirely.

And that was the thing that had stopped him. Had made him hesitate for a second when he reached the frightened female facing off against Morthil. Made him pause for a breath before interjecting.

He had suspected, in his dragon shape. He hadn't known it was possible, but a part of him had wondered.

But now… now that he had shifted into his own human shape.

He knew.

She was his.

The one female destiny had given him. The one that would be his match, his mirror, the single being that could withstand even his hottest flames, for she was a part of him. The one that was meant to belong to him and only him. The one that might end his unending boredom.

His twin flame.

His fated mate.

"I do not belong to you." Her eyes glinted up at him.

He hadn't been able to stop himself from going closer. He wanted to breathe in her scent. He wanted to mix it with his own.

At her words, he smiled. But it was less a warm shape and more a bearing of teeth. "I disagree. And in these caves, my word is law, female."

"I have a name, you know."

He shrugged, as though he was not suddenly desperate to learn it. "I suppose you do. But it was you who was not polite enough to introduce yourself after I did just that for myself and the swallump."

He kept his face straight even as he saw a dozen replies play on her lips. Oh, it had hardly been a slight to not introduce herself—she'd been paralyzed with fear. By a baby swallump!

But it was fun to rile her up.

"My name is Nora—Lenora," she corrected herself, "Tashe of Mossley Village."

"Lenora Tashe." He enjoyed the shape of her name on his lips, but in his own ears, all he heard was *mine*.

Oh, but it would not be enough to simply own her. To keep her as part of his hoard in body only. No, he would have every inch of her, every part of her. He would learn it. He would make her share it of her own volition.

Nothing less was acceptable.

Alistair did not often deal with living things he was not in the process of terrorizing or consuming. But no matter—he would call on his limited experience. Morthil would be his inspiration.

"Do you desire food, Lenora Tashe?"

The frown that quirked on her luscious lips said she would deny it for spite, before she hesitated and then thought better of it.

A reluctant nod was all the invitation he needed.

In an effort to be gallant, he extended an arm to her.

She looked at it as though it might burn her.

"Won't you put something on?" she asked, meeting his eyes with a delicious flush that crept up her neck.

He frowned at her. "Why should I? You humans wear things to keep safe from the cold; I have no such defect."

Her lips thinned into a line matched by her narrowed eyes, but she didn't argue. After a moment's internal debate, she took his extended arm.

*Victory.*

The first of many to come.

Truth be told, Alistair normally enjoyed wearing the fine clothes he collected in the solitude of his home.

But it was much more fun to pretend otherwise. Especially when his female couldn't help but react to him, the blush that reached all the way down to her throat beckoning him.

He knew his body was perfection, by dragon and by human standards. All he had to do was stand in front of her for a bit and no doubt she would fall into his lap.

If she would just look at him. The stubborn thing seemed determined to avoid examining him.

It would hardly do. They were fated mates, cursed and blessed to learn each other's souls, as well as their bodies.

While he guided her deeper into the caves, he stole glances at her. She was slight, in all ways compared to him, but he found he enjoyed that. He liked the delicate little thing. She would need his protection.

She would be his to keep.

She gasped when they reached what passed for his kitchen.

He didn't spend much time in his human shape, certainly not to eat, so it was not the most extensive part of his hoard. Fourteen identical golden chairs lined a long table. There were enchanted cupboards in the wall, a token from one of the magical outposts.

"Are all of those *gold*?"

Good. His mate should appreciate his hoard. He puffed his chest as he replied, "Indeed."

"How wasteful!"

That wiped the smile off Alistair's face.

"This could feed Mossley for *centuries*."

"It does not belong to Mossley," he snapped at the rebuke. "It belongs to *me*." *As do you.*

His mate would need to understand. A dragon's power came from his hoard. A dragon did not share. A dragon did not so much as like to speculate about being separated from a single coin in his hoard, let alone a furniture set.

Her gaze was full of censure, *not* understanding.

Fine. He would brush that aside for now.

Feed her. Creatures learned to yield to the hand that fed them.

He pulled some victuals from the shelf. Cured meats seemed the most suitable, so he prepared a plate and brought it over to the table, along with a glass of wine he had not bothered to try yet. His mate had settled at the far end, Morthil at her heels. No matter how she edged her seat away, he simply lifted his hindquarters, inched forward, and settled back down.

Eventually, she gave up the battle.

Alistair laughed as he placed the plate down in the spot next to her, where he settled in.

"You will have no success dissuading him. Once he settles his heart on something, he does not deviate." Something he found he had in common with the pup.

Lenora glanced down at the creature, who looked up at her, pleading for acceptance. She patted his head for the second time, albeit only slightly less reluctantly than before.

"Eat, Lenora."

She turned back to him and frowned at his outstretched fingers.

"You must be joking."

Alistair frowned. He'd hoped to have her take from his hand, to feel her lips against his skin. "I'm not."

"I'm not going to eat like an animal from your hand." Her horror overpowered the fear that had seeped back into her composure.

It was enough to make Alistair drop the matter, even if he was slightly disappointed.

*Another time*, he promised himself.

"Very well."

Her suspicion was obvious as she pulled the plate close, but hunger won out. He tossed the offending piece of meat over to Morthil, who swallowed it in one gulp.

It was enough for him to know that no matter how many barriers she erected, they were inevitable. Even if his mate was not aware of that fact quite yet.

Just the thought of her eventually yielding to his every demand sent a bolt of lust straight through him, hardening his length. At least it was hidden by the table. Not that Alistair felt any shame in his desire; no, he had cause for pride in that regard. But given his fated mate and future wife's propensity towards screaming, it was better she not see—yet.

Better to distract himself.

"Come, pet." He enjoyed the flicker of annoyance in her eyes at the term. "Converse with me. Entertain your master."

"If you call yourself my master again, I'll... I'll starve myself."

Ah, but she did not know what he did. She was his mate. He was her master, like it or not. Alistair could not contain his grin.

If she did not want to face the realities of her situation yet, so be it. He didn't want to break his new toy. He could woo with honey as easily as demand.

"Would you deny a lonely dragon the gift of your conversation?"

His female was likely stubborn enough to keep silent for spite, but when he preyed on her kinder nature?

"I'm surprised you have food for... people," Nora eventually relented.

"In fact, I keep it only for Morthil. This would hardly satisfy me."

"Great. I'm eating cat food. Or your equivalent of it."

"Swallumps *do* have discerning palates."

"That makes me feel *so* much better." Her droll tone pleased him. He would not do well with a female that lacked a sharp wit. "So what do you sate your hunger with then? Livestock?"

"I wouldn't say I'm often *sated*."

She blushed, turning her cheeks a bright pink. Oh, he enjoyed the heat on her cheeks. He wanted to press his own hand against it, but the feisty thing might nip his fingers.

Perhaps all the more reason...

"Do you eat... people?" she asked quickly.

"I'm certainly capable of it." She shrank, but held his gaze. "But I would not choose to unless I had need. I'm partial to mutton, personally. Humans are far too stringy for my taste."

When she did not look relieved, he added, "That was a joke, Lenora."

It was not a joke, but she relaxed nonetheless.

"Tell me, pretty one, how did you come to be so lucky as to be chosen for me?"

Her blush grew from pink to scarlet. At this, her gaze did fall away. Not fear. Embarrassment.

The thought of being gobbled whole by him was less worrisome to her than admitting how she had come to be in the situation.

Oh, Alistair had to know now. "Come now, Lenora. It cannot be so awful. Even if you robbed a priest or killed a man, it would hardly register to me."

"I'm not a criminal!" Offended, she forgot her embarrassment and those bright blue eyes found him for a beat before she looked away. "You could say it was not anything I did, but what I didn't do."

He waited for her to go on.

"There's a woman in our village. She calls herself a seer, though we all think she's batty. But this time, for some reason, they took her seriously. I think my stepmother was just glad to be rid of me when I fit the conditions. One less mouth to feed, after all. The farm hasn't produced much, especially not since the floods last season."

"And what condition was this?" he prodded when she said no more. They were fools to part with her. Fools, or desperate, because anyone could see what a jewel the female was. Not just her looks, which could have been lifted from any one of the portraits of beautiful goddesses he kept in his hoard. But for everything else about her—her wit, her kindness, her courage.

"I... I am untouched. And the seer said such a sacrifice would be worth more than the prearranged fifteen sheep."

She did not meet his gaze, and he found that intolerable. He tilted her head towards him with one black claw.

"The seer had a point. I'm a dragon, after all. It's not in my nature to share. Though I imagine I would be pleased with you regardless, so long as you know no male shall touch you ever again."

Her flush grew. She lifted the glass of wine for cover. "They thought you were going to eat me."

"Oh, I plan to," he said. "I intend to feast on your body, Lenora, just not the way your village expected."

She looked at him for a moment, as if confused. Then, the meaning slamming into her, she jerked back in her seat and dropped her goblet, splashing bright wine all over her dirty frock.

"Oh, blight!" His female turned her attention to the ruined frock, and he allowed the distraction. "I guess the downside of not being eaten is I didn't bring any supplies of my own."

*Fear not,* Alistair thought. *I will see you in clothes far finer than you could imagine.*

But first...

"I believe, then, it's time for you to bathe."

# Chapter 5

THE DRAGON SEEMED TO delight in Lenora's misfortune and wasted no time shepherding her deeper into the caves.

She searched for any discarded scales from the corner of her eye as they walked through the winding path, but her thoughts were clouded by his words. Oh, he seemed to delight in taunting her.

And the last thing Alistair had said, which had caused her to spill the wine she'd been sipping for relief—she found herself quite parched in the dragon's presence! Oh, it had taken her a moment. To realize he was not threatening to devour her like livestock, but in another way altogether.

The path grew darker and darker, the torches unlit. She was focused on clinging to him for guidance, lest she stumble on the uneven pathway he had no trouble with.

Worse, he remained nude, without a speck of shame. Perhaps he saw himself as nothing but a beast, rendering clothes useless.

But he wore the shape of a man. A very large man... in every regard. And it did nothing to ease her mind.

The only respite was the beast, Morthil, had not followed them further.

"Here we are."

They were in a space no less black than it had been a moment before.

"Are you not pleased?" Alistair asked when she was silent. If she was a buffoon, she might have thought he sounded almost hurt that she did not like it.

"Alistair, I cannot see."

"Ah!" A breath later, the room was lit in the low yellows of flame. "I like hearing you say my name. Do it more," he commanded.

She rolled her eyes. He was a vain creature, no doubt, but if she wanted to survive long enough to enact her plan, she'd best humor him.

"Alistair, it's the grandest thing I've ever seen." And this was no exaggeration.

There was a pool of water, carved from crystal, buried in the ground. The torch flames bounced off the stone, revealing the shape, which was maybe the size of a small animal enclosure in the village. Clear water reflected back the light. It went all the way until a far cave wall, which was inlaid with shelves full of crystalline bottles that belonged to the sort far too wealthy to ever even visit Mossley.

"Good. Get in it."

Lenora startled and faced him. "Surely you would leave me to bathe in privacy."

The smirk that teased at his lips was nothing less than roguish. "Surely I would not."

"It's improper!"

But Alistair only laughed. Dragons, obviously, had no idea of the rules of propriety.

"You came here prepared to die, and yet the idea of bathing while I'm here is too much?"

"Yes," she hissed.

"Come now, surely turnabout is fair play." He gestured to himself.

"If it was up to me, you would be clothed, not walking around like an animal who knows no better," she snapped. It was very hard not to look down at that moment.

"You don't like what you see?"

She flushed. The issue was she very much did, more than she'd liked anything or anyone ever before. And the grin on the beast's face said he guessed as much.

"Very well, I shall leave." His voice was soft, conciliatory. "Though, of course, you won't fault Morthil if he decides to hop in alongside you. If I'm not here to stop him, well, he can hardly be expected to know better."

She had petted the creature. Twice. And it reminded her of that old barn cat. It was probably even harmless.

But the idea of it jumping in while she was vulnerable... she shivered. "Fine. Suit yourself."

The unbidden glee on Alistair's face said he'd expected no less from her answer.

"Will you at least turn around?" she asked, exasperated.

Alistair complied without a word. She quickly shucked off her clothes and set them at the very edge of the pool and moved into the water, turning away from the dragon so she would not be distracted while she bathed.

He had a very distracting backside.

It was a bit chilly, but Lenora hadn't had the luxury of a full bath in some years, so she decided to be grateful for it. She unwound her hair from the plaits atop her head and tried to adjust to the temperature.

Until there was another plop in the water.

He didn't...

But when she turned around, startled, there was Alistair.

She opened her mouth to chide him, to argue, to tell him it was absolutely improper for him to be in there with her and to shriek and anything else that might keep him away from her while she stood up to her shoulders in crystal-clear water when the most marvelous thing happened.

The water grew warm.

Not just lukewarm. No, the temperature rose and rose until it was very nearly hot.

It was the most glorious thing Lenora had ever experienced. In Mossley, she only got the used water after her stepmother finished, as it was too much work to haul enough for two. Bathing was always a tepid, brisk affair. Functional. As far as her stepmother went, those tepid baths were a kindness compared to the rest of her treatment.

But this?

This was *pleasure*.

A moan escaped her lips before she could call it back.

Alistair's gaze had fixed on her with a mischievous grin, but at the sound, it turned predatory. His eyes narrowed slightly, and he took a step through the water towards her.

She moved back.

He moved forward.

Back.

Forward.

A dance until her back was pressed against the crystalline wall. He reached for her. Fear and anticipation twirled in her belly. She couldn't stop him, couldn't force this powerful male to stay his hand.

But instead of grabbing her, he reached past her head, pulled something from the shelf, and handed her a bottle.

She blinked at it for a moment, then, with tentative hands, accepted it. The graze of flesh was electric. Was this some dragon magic, wanting him so much?

Inside the glass container was bathing oil, perfumed in a lovely way that made Lenora want to sigh. Nothing like the scents she'd been accustomed to on the farm, of manure and dirt that clung to her even after she washed.

"I... I can't."

"Use another if that one isn't to your liking," Alistair instructed. "Use them all."

"Something like this is too fine for me," she protested.

"Nothing is too fine for you," he replied in a gravelly voice.

Lenora shivered despite the warm water. "Aren't dragons supposed to jealously guard their treasure?"

He moved closer, caging her in with his arms on either side. There was enough space between them that they did not touch. And not a thread's breadth more.

"*You* are my treasure." The words were powerful, daring her to argue. "You're my pet after all."

She hated it when he called her a pet.

But when he did it in *that* tone, low, sensual... blight take her if she didn't feel the words deep in her center.

"You should clean me with it first if you have such an issue." The gleam in his eye said he expected her to fluster as she constantly did around him.

"Fine."

For the first time since she'd met him, Alistair was the one to startle, his eyes flaring in surprise at her quick agreement.

But she agreed for two reasons. First of all, if she cleaned him, his back would be towards her and she could escape that mesmerizing gray gaze.

And second—and it should've mattered less, yet it had been the true reason she agreed—being an innocent had gotten her into this mess, after all. And while she would certainly never actually lie with the beast, especially not spread for him to feast as he'd implied, she was curious. No one would ever know.

Either because when she triumphed and returned to the village a hero, she would never tell. Or, in all likelihood, if she failed to kill him, he would slaughter her in turn and it would not matter.

And hadn't she vowed to herself, for just that reason, that she would not fear him?

This should be no different.

She poured the oil between her hands and slowly, gently, laid a palm on his back.

When the world did not explode into flames on the spot, she began to move across his shoulder, feeling the corded muscles beneath her fingers. She poured more oil and set the bottle down, moving both hands to massage and clean him.

Slowly she grew bolder. He didn't push for more than she would give; he didn't shirk from her touch.

She moved from his shoulders, down his back. He turned for her to touch his front. Her breath hitched at the look in his eyes. They were almost entirely black, so dark she couldn't tell where the pupil ended and the iris began.

Her fingers drifted across his chest while she held his gaze. When they stumbled over a nipple, Alistair groaned, breaking the spell of silence, his eyes briefly closing at the sensation.

Nora had never heard such an erotic sound. Her fingers stilled, and when his eyes reopened, there was a command there.

But somehow the sound had broken the spell. She still wanted to touch him, but it was too much.

"There's more of me to clean." His voice was little more than a whisper, but the sound could not be described as soft.

She huffed and pulled her hands away. "I shall go no lower."

That would infuriate the dragon, no doubt. The beast who was never told no. She was defenseless against him, but she took her stand all the same, bracing for his fury.

But as ever, Alistair didn't react with any of the brutishness she expected. He simply grinned in a way that told her she had played into the palm of his hand, yet again.

"Then it's my turn."

Her breath caught, the words sending a jolt that made her feel even more vulnerable than the nudity.

But Alistair didn't move for her. Instead, despite his confident words, the silent question hung in his eyes.

Would she allow this?

It had been one thing to touch him. It was another to be touched, to give him that power over her.

But there was no one here to see, no one to ever know and shame her.

She plucked an oil from the shelf, handed it to him on shaky fingers, and turned around. Then, to convince him as much as herself that she was ready for this, she brushed her long locks from her neck and exposed her back to him so he could begin.

No touch came.

Confused, Nora turned back to face the dragon.

If she thought his eyes before smoldered with desire, now it was gone, replaced with fury.

On instinct, she tried to move back, but his hands snapped out, clawed fingertips digging into her shoulder as he held her in place.

"Who did this to you?"

## Chapter 6

SOMEONE HAD MARKED HIS mate.

Someone had dared to touch what belonged to him.

His female had blushed at the confession that no one had ever touched her sexually. Alistair enjoyed the knowledge he would educate her in this, but it made no difference.

But this? Someone would die for this.

"You're hurting me. Alistair!" she yelped.

He immediately released her shoulders. Still, the anger rolled off of him. He wanted to roar. Wanted to find whoever had done this. And he wouldn't simply end them. He would make them beg for it before he was through.

"The water is getting too hot!"

He forced himself to tamp down on his anger, dousing his power, lest he boil his fated mate in this very pool.

"Tell me, Lenora. Who dared harm you like that?"

It was an effort to speak quietly when he ached to roar at the injustice. But he didn't want to terrify the female any more than he already had.

Her back was covered in scars. He was no expert in human wounds, for his own body didn't scar and no one had landed a blow on him in decades, but there was no mistaking the fact they must have been excruciating. Lines across her back, some newer, some old and faded. She was young, his mate.

She would've been a child when someone had hurt her.

Oh, they would rue the day they first thought to take a hand to an obsidian dragon's twin flame.

"It doesn't matter." She wouldn't meet his gaze.

"If it doesn't, then you will tell me."

"Why, so you can eat her?"

*Her.* That narrowed it down to perhaps half the pathetic humans in his Lenora's little village.

"I will not eat her," he promised.

Eating someone was an effective way of dealing with enemies, but it was too quick. Often the neck was snapped by the time they made their way down his throat, or simply dissolved in his stomach acid. Too pleasant for what Alistair had in mind.

"Then it doesn't matter, does it?" His courageous mate had returned.

Ah, but her loyalty was misdirected, and that infuriated Alistair anew.

"You will tell me how you came to have these scars, Lenora. Because if you do not, I shall fly to Mossley and set the entire town alight. In fact, since I hardly know one settlement from another, I may paint this entire country in flames. Surely you do not want that."

She gaped at him. "You would kill thousands! Hundreds of thousands."

He looked at her, taking in every curve of her face, the wide set of her eyes, the way the hair framed her face. As if any of them mattered, even all summed together, when weighed against his fated one.

"Come now, pretty one," he coaxed. "One life for so many. They made the same trade for you, didn't they?" Perhaps it was cruel to pour salt into that particular ache, but he needed the name.

She hesitated. Alistair could feel her indecision, weighing whether his words were simply an empty threat. They weren't, but it would be much more satisfying for him to hunt down the particular offender.

"I can't." The words broke from her lips, forced out in an uneven space.

He forced himself to rein in the desire to push more. Their bond was young; she did not trust him yet, but in time, she would. And then he would have vengeance on her behalf. Whoever had dared lift a whip to his mate was marked for a painful death. But for now, more important than that, was comforting his mate.

"I'm sorry," she continued. "Please don't destroy Wyrdova."

He would burn the world for her in a heartbeat. But not if the thought brought her pain.

"Hush now, pretty one. I'm not going anywhere."

"Pretty." She scoffed. "With my skin so ruined."

"There's not a single part of you that could *ever* be ruined."

"You can't expect me to believe you could find my body pleasing like this."

He drew closer. "Does it please me to know someone dare harmed my"—he nearly said mate, but quickly adjusted—"treasure? Of course not. But you could never be made lesser by someone's acts against you. They should be worn with honor. You are not defined by someone's cruelty; you are defined by your strength for overcoming their trespasses."

She watched him carefully. He wished he could feel her emotions more fully, the way truly bonded twin flames could. Wished he could know what she was thinking. But that would not come for some time, not until she let him into her heart.

At last, a small measure of tension eased from her shoulders.

"And no one will ever do that again," he finished with a growl. The urge to turn into a dragon and hunt down whoever might have harmed his female, to prove the truth in his words and eliminate any threats, was overwhelming, but no. That wasn't what mattered now.

"Do they hurt?" The idea of his mate in pain was unbearable.

"Not often," Lenora admitted. Which meant they hurt more often than he liked.

"Then let me make it better."

He retook the oil, and after a moment's hesitation, she obediently turned for him.

When he'd first demanded she bathe him, he'd told himself it was a joke. A bit of teasing to get a reaction from the bashful female. He had not wanted to admit, even to himself, how badly he had craved to feel her hands on him.

No one had properly touched him in centuries. Even Morthil seldom lowered himself to come to be petted, and that suited Alistair fine.

But his mate... he had wanted to beg for her touch. When she gave it, he thought he had found a pleasure even greater than flying beneath a moonlit sky. Yet her touch became torture, because Alistair was determined to not touch her back. He didn't dare startle her cautious exploration. It had been a wonder, to see her grow more confident, to enjoy learning her mate's body. His muscles had tensed with need, but he'd stilled his hands.

Now, his patience was rewarded.

Her skin was soft to the touch, like the smoothest silk he'd ever been offered. Few of the scars were raised on her back after so long, and though it threatened to set Alistair's rage alight again, he controlled himself for her sake.

Her muscles were tense, stiff from the journey. He used the oil to massage them, not bothering with the pretense of cleaning. He enjoyed her natural scent, berries and springtime, able to breathe it in now that he could bury his head in her hair.

Yet there was an eroticism to using the oil, part of his hoard, to spoil her. A hoard was seldom meant to be used. It was to be owned, acquired, put on a shelf.

But her... oh he had meant what he said. He would not rest until he had tried every single perfume and cosmetic and saw how it mingled with her scent.

As the knots released from her shoulders, he began to move his hands to the front, but stayed them, waiting for protest.

None came. Instead, the barest dip of her head, a silent approval he might have missed if not for his perfect vision.

*Finally.*

# Chapter 7

ALISTAIR COULD HAVE DONE anything, taken anything from Lenora, and she would have been powerless to stop him.

Yet he waited. He constantly asked, and despite his demanding nature, he listened. She would deter him from his vendetta against her stepmother, but at the moment, such thoughts were far, far away.

His touch was perfection.

She had thought the hot bath was good. His hands were otherworldly. They were warm, a shade shy of too hot, and just the contact was soothing.

But the movement?

It sent static all over her, putting every part of her on edge.

She leaned back against his chest as he moved his hands over her body. She could *feel* him peering down at her, feel his hungry eyes on her. Lenora had never given much thought to her appearance; boys in the village had flirted but none had been besotted, and she seldom saw a reflective surface long enough to form an opinion.

But his gaze made her feel powerful.

For he was obsessed with her.

*He's a dragon,* she tried to chide herself. *He thinks you belong to him, and he likes to collect things no matter whom it harms.*

But it was impossible to remember that logic when he touched her like that.

His hands moved around the swells of her breasts, kneading the flesh. He'd startled her when he'd grabbed her before, but now? His touch was gentle yet demanding. Demanding she yield.

She was caged between his chest and hands, yet she'd never felt safer.

His grip shifted. He took one peak between two fingers and rolled it.

She moaned. If she could have moved her arms, she'd have covered her mouth for shame, but it wasn't possible.

At the sound, she felt a sudden jerk behind her. Her flush grew when she realized what it was. Alistair's length pressed against her, and though it should terrify her, she found herself intrigued.

*But I'll never know.* That would be too far for her.

He continued to massage her breasts, spicing the sensation when he twisted and tugged on her nipples. Her breath came faster until she was gasping at every touch. Alistair was unhurried in his movements, yet he was also unrelenting, not giving her a moment to compose herself.

She wriggled in his grasp, unsure what she was reaching for, but the sensation sent his length directly between her. In combination with his insistent touches, the pleasure grew and grew. Lenora had never felt such a thing before, felt as though she were drawing closer to some edge she couldn't yet see over.

He adjusted her in his arms, one fluid movement moving her so she directly faced the beast while perched upon his knee that settled between her thighs. Only he wasn't a beast in her eyes, not at this moment. He wore the shape of a man, and he wore it expertly. As expertly as he used his hands to continue to touch, to stroke the pleasure that built inside her core.

And then he leaned in as if to kiss her.

For a moment—the briefest second—she leaned in, under his spell.

Then she jerked back.

"No."

Alistair paused, fingers frozen in place. "No?"

She shook her head. No. She couldn't do this. Couldn't kiss the dragon and then stab him in his slumber.

She braced for anger—even the boys in the village got nasty when they felt they'd been denied after some flirting, and surely a dragon had a worse temper than that—but he simply nodded and eased away from her.

"I'll fetch you something to change into."

She wanted to open her mouth to apologize, to comfort him for some inexplicable reason. To explain, even if such an explanation damned her.

But he was gone too quickly. In the span of a few seconds, he swam across the pool and exited. To punish herself, she didn't let her gaze follow his magnificent form and instead finished washing before returning to the edge of the pool. Frustration replaced the pleasure he'd built, souring in her stomach as she crossed her arms over her tender chest.

Alistair reappeared with a pile of clothes, gold thread glinting off the dim light. He'd also put on a pair of trousers, a fine cut that clung low on his hips, the drawstring untied.

"Come, pretty one. It's time to slumber."

Deeper and deeper they went into the caves. Morthil met them part way through, and in her exhausted state, she found the abominable creature to be a comfort.

Nora thought she had seen the sum of his hoard above, where golden furniture lined the walls and piles of books, clothing, and all manner of wealth littered the room. It was more than she had ever thought a person could own.

But then as they continued deeper, they reached Alistair's true hoard.

It was more than she had ever imagined a dragon could own.

Piles and piles of gold filled the large cavern. Chunks and coins and bars made mountains that glittered in firelight, which accented the gemstones contained within the piles, like garlands around the yuletide thistles.

She froze at the entryway, awestruck. For it was not just blatant wealth, but also artistry. Paintings of every type—some masterful in depictions, some crude—sculptures, instruments, more and more books, furniture.

Alistair did not interrupt her lollygagging. When she finally turned her attention back to him, he grinned, a self-satisfied smirk on his lips.

He liked to see her impressed, she had come to realize. Perhaps it was a lonely thing, to own so much and have no one to share it with.

Of course, he wasn't truly sharing it. He considered her as much of a possession as the emerald in a nearby pile.

It was hard to know if she should be flattered or offended anymore. If she was safe and desired, or at his peril.

Both, in all likelihood.

"I will sleep here," she declared, moving towards a magnificent four-poster bed. The wood was expertly carved; a far cry from the little spot by her stepmother's hearth she had claimed for herself, where the dirt had been softened and she used the dishrags as a pillow.

Alistair voiced no disapproval, so she moved forward. She was tired, but she had work to do this evening, after her captor slumbered.

Unable to stop herself, she glanced back at him, guilt pricking her stomach.

And this was how she learned that it was a silent thing for him to turn back into a humongous dragon.

Before she could protest, he lifted her in one massive claw, flapped over the ground, and settled onto the largest pile of gold at the very center of the room. It had been so large that Nora had not been able to even see the top.

He curved his body around the golden mountain, settling his wings.

And as if she were another emerald, he placed her at the top.

"Alistair, you can't mean for me to sleep here."

He did not look at her, simply closed his eyes. But surely he heard her.

"It may be comfortable for you, a great scaly beast, to sleep atop this mountain, but I'm more likely to slide off it and break my back," she complained. Plus, it would make it harder to look for discarded scales.

A single gray eye opened, considering. Then, he extended a claw and let her down. This time he didn't clutch her so much as let her hang on as he gently lowered her.

Now to find her bed again. She bit down on a laugh. How easy to think of this impossible wealth as hers. *How foolish.*

Yet Alistair did not settle back to sleep. He rose off the pile and flew to different corners of the cavern, lifting items and flying back to the apex of the golden mountain while Nora searched for the bed.

No sooner had she found it than those massive claws came back to grab her.

And this time she was not set atop the tallest mountain of gold ever conceived.

No, she was placed with a soft thump on a pile of fur-lined coats and tapestries and silk shirts and embroidered dresses and down blankets which was atop the tallest mountain of gold she'd ever seen.

It was soft, softer than even her stepmother's bed had been the few times she'd risked a nap somewhere other than her spot by the hearth. She rolled back before she could stop herself, spreading out in glee.

It was so comfortable! Like a cloud or dandelion fluff.

Even with the giant, self-satisfied gray eye glaring down at her, she felt as though she might fall asleep for a hundred years.

His draconic body curved around her, even closer than before, the heat from his scales erasing the chill that seeped into her bones.

"Does you have to sleep like that?" she muttered, mostly because she wanted to find something to hate about a beast who bathed her in fine perfumes, dressed her in finer clothes, and made a bed for her worth more than she could earn in a hundred lifetimes.

"I could wrap myself around you in my human shape if you prefer."

Her jaw flew open. "You can talk as a dragon?"

"I am always a dragon. But yes, I can speak when I take this shape."

"But... but I've never heard of that."

He huffed, a billow of smoke flaring up from his nostrils. "Humans are seldom worthy conversation companions."

Now it was her turn to huff. "I suppose I should be flattered then."

"You should be," he agreed easily. "You're special, Lenora Tashe."

It was an effort not to scoff. She was nothing special. She was worth so little her stepmother had jumped at the chance to sacrifice her.

Her morose thoughts were interrupted by soft flapping as Morthil crested over the mountain and settled into the pile next to her.

She wanted to protest, to complain. But when it curled into a ball, a mere arm's breadth away, looking at her with pleading eyes before tucking himself away, she found herself reaching to stroke him. Not just for his comfort, but for hers.

By the time the snoring started from the dragon, she very nearly ceded herself to sleep.

Blight, it had been an exhausting day. Filled with horrors, and somehow also unexpected delights, which were their own manner of terror. All at once, it took its toll and Nora wanted nothing more than to rest.

But no. She had to do this. Had to fulfill the prophecy Crazy Bess had told her and slay the dragon, earning her place as a respected, valued member of Mossley—or die trying.

Likely die trying.

But one thing was to be certain, it *had* to be tonight. If she didn't do so soon, if she let him continue to treat her like a cherished pet, she might find it impossible. She couldn't allow her resolve to weaken with time.

She had to find a scale.

All evening she had scoured the cave, searching for any sign. But perhaps dragons did not shed scales as easily as she shed her hair.

It was hard to see in the dim light. The obsidian scales curved around her, nearly absorbing the light as they shone slightly.

And yet... there was one that was not as even with the others. One that poked out. She moved slowly, so as to not disturb Morthil, and took a closer look.

A smaller scale grew, edging out the other, larger one.

She steadied her breath, barely able to hear over the roaring of her heart.

Alistair still slept; his snores were loud and impossible to miss.

Slowly, barely moving, she extended her arms and gripped either side of the scale. The edge was sharp like a blade. She moved it back and forth.

And then, at last, it was loose.

She froze in place, listening.

Still, the dragon slumbered.

The scale itself was the size of her two hands together across and slightly longer at the top. She clutched it to her chest.

She could hardly use it as it was. She would need to fashion a spear; she had seen holy carved lances in the hoard.

Getting down was not so simple. Doing it silently, even less so. But somehow she managed and crept through the cavern. She found the wooden base for her spear and fashioned the scale to it, cutting fabric from the strip of her gown in order to do so.

Guilt crawled over her skin. It felt wrong to do this after the bath they'd shared.

But she had no choice. She had to kill the dragon that had tormented Wyrdova for decades. For her village.

For her to finally belong.

It would have been better if her fingers shook around the makeshift spear. If her body betrayed the indecision that tumbled back and forth in her head. But her body was strong from years of laboring for her stepmother, and her grip did not err.

She crept back to the golden mountain. The dragon was so large its chest rested only a bit off the ground even as its back reached the very top.

She maneuvered until she was above where she expected the dragon's heart to be. All the while, he slumbered, unaware that she was about to end his eternal life.

Before she could give herself more time to hesitate, she thrust the spear directly into his chest.

## Chapter 8

ALISTAIR WAS A DEEP sleeper. Once he settled down for the evening, he normally did not rouse until many hours later. Yet he was hardly rested as he awoke.

Something was itching at his chest. A giant gnat some witch had conjured to sting him, perhaps?

He flicked his eyes open.

In front of him was his female. Awake, not asleep even after he had so thoughtfully arranged a bed for her, one suitable for his twin flame.

When their gazes connected, she stumbled back and tripped over herself.

The itch on his chest persisted. He craned his massive neck and looked down.

There, protruding from his armored skin, was a pole. It could hardly be called a weapon, but it was immediately obvious what had happened.

The chit had tried to kill him.

Blessed flame knew it was impossible, the way she'd gone about it, but she likely didn't know. She had actually tried to end him.

It was, perhaps, the bravest thing his little female had ever done. Utterly stupid—if you're going to kill someone, you'd best be certain—but he respected it. However misguided she had been, his mate was a fierce thing, and it did him proud to call her his own.

Then the female got up and began to flee, nearly tripping herself again in the process.

An attempt on his life? Good-natured fun. A bit of amusement he welcomed after his boring existence.

But to flee from him, her fated connection?

Now that *annoyed* him.

It was a matter of seconds to fly after his female, who again, to her credit, did not scream, even as she thrashed about when he trapped her beneath his claws, caging her against the ground.

It was barely another breath for him to turn to his human shape and roll over her, his hands shackling her own to the ground while his hips pinned her legs open even as the skirts blocked him from feeling her silk-soft flesh against him.

He bent forward. And because—no matter how humorous her failed assassination attempt was—he couldn't let her attempt to flee go unpunished. He nipped at her earlobe.

"I will tolerate much from you," he purred. "But leaving me? Unacceptable. I'm going to make it so you never dare leave me again."

"Are you going to hurt me?" Her voice quivered.

"Never, precious one. I'm going to make you feel so good that you never dream of leaving my protection again."

Her pulse jumped at his words.

The urge to claim her rolled through him. He wanted to burn himself on her then and there, but he wasn't a brute. Right now, fear and desire warred within his mate. It was his sacred duty to ensure desire won.

"Oh, you like the sound of that. Tell me, Lenora, are you writhing under me because you're still making a futile attempt to escape, or because you know it makes my cock hard?"

Her gasp was everything Alistair had ever dreamed.

"I think the latter," he continued. "I think you like knowing the effect you have on your male."

"Mine?" she repeated.

She liked that, did she? Good. Because they would be bound together. He would make it so she could never bear to part with him.

"Yours." He nuzzled her neck, tasting her scent. "And you're mine."

With that, he finally claimed her lips. The lips that had taunted, teased, tested him since he'd first spotted her.

His press was insistent, but not yet demanding. His mate had never known a male's touch, and he had time to savor her surrender. Her lips tasted like berries, and he licked them, coaxing her to let him inside.

Hesitantly, they parted. Alistair took that for the gift it was and deepened the kiss, guiding his mate. Her hands were still caged above her, but no longer did she try to pull away. Instead, she strained as she tasted him in turn, learning the shape of him.

His cock was hard, aching for attention, but he refused to rush the task. He let her do her study, then began to devour her in truth.

When they finally parted for breath, she gazed up at him with a wanton expression that nearly made him give seed then and there.

"I'm... I'm sorry I tried to kill you," she whimpered.

He grinned down at her. "That, I hardly mind. Wound me any way you wish, Lenora Tashe, and I shall accept it as my due. But you apologize still for the wrong thing. It seems I have a lesson to teach you."

## Chapter 9

Lenora didn't know what to make of the beast above her. When she'd failed, she'd thought her life was over.

Now, she suspected she hadn't been alive at all. Not until he'd kissed her and awoken her soul.

It was impossible to catch her breath as she looked up at him. He was nude, having transformed from the great beast that had pinned her between his claws into a male that now held her body in place with frightening ease.

But worst of all wasn't his physical strength. It was that seductive nature when her name rolled off his tongue, sounding elegant, sounding precious, like a jewel in his hoard, as he trapped her there with nothing more than words and a kiss.

"You told me you had never had a male before."

Unsure what to do, she nodded. Even now, she flushed from this. At least it would blend with the rest of her blushes that now coated her cheeks.

"I should like to change that tonight." His voice was a soft, dark promise, yet again he made no move. Waiting.

Did she want him? It had felt like a worse betrayal, to touch him and then destroy him. But she had failed. Now, she had no chance at killing the beast that terrorized Mossley and finding refuge there after. He would be on guard and not allow her to make a second attempt.

Now, there was no reason to deny herself.

She nodded.

Alistair did not move, not for three more breaths while he considered her. As if he was waiting to see if she would change her mind.

But she would not. As strange as it was, he had made her feel less judged than those in her village, who were of her species.

And when he kissed her again, there could be no other explanation than that he was otherworldly. No man should be able to make a woman so breathless, so weak, so alive, with just a kiss.

Nor should he be so skilled with his hands.

With a seemingly careless swipe, he shredded the front of her tunic, nails trailing over her skin without so much as scratching her. She bared herself for him, and he moved that same hand to her breast, fondling them as he had in the tub.

And then, when her nipples grew stiff and aching, he lowered his mouth to one and sucked.

Nora moaned, unable and unwilling to muffle the sound.

"Make that sound again, precious one," he instructed.

And then he drew it from her again. She couldn't have disobeyed if she'd even wanted to. Her hands instinctively threaded through his obsidian locks and held him as he sucked at her bosom. His other hand let go of her wrists and went lower, lower, lifting the skirts even farther past where they'd rode up.

She tensed, even amidst the pleasure. No one had ever touched her there. Alistair simply waited, patiently urging her to yield to him while he continued to sow pleasure with his lips.

Her body eased and his fingers lifted to her center, finding her wet. Wetter than she had ever been when she woke from lustful dreams that kept her warm when the hearth failed.

Then he lifted the finger to his mouth.

Seeing his intent, she gasped. "You can't."

A cunning expression flitted across Alistair's face. "Why? Would you rather taste how much you desire me?"

He extended the finger towards her lips, barely an inch away.

It felt dirty. Lewd. Yet she licked her lips at the thought.

But before she could close the distance, he retracted the offer and pulled it to his own lips, tapping the claw against them. "Not this time, Lenora. I'm a greedy dragon. I won't allow you to rob me of your pleasure."

Then he sucked it clean. His gray eyes lit with pleasure, pupils flaring in delight, which made Nora grow hot to see. "Delicious."

She groaned, shifting against him for friction. She had never seen such an erotic sight.

"I think I'll take another taste," he informed her with a purr.

But he didn't move his hand back to her center. Instead, he moved over her body, his naked muscles gliding over her with heated pressure as he moved his head to the apex of her thighs.

And then he tasted her.

Pleasure ricocheted through her body and she wasn't able to stop the sound she made. She moved her hands from his hair to cover her face, as if to hide from her dragon lover, even as he licked her lower mound and made her buck her hips.

He moved from her thighs, long enough to take her hands away and hold himself close enough to kiss her jaw.

"I told you, Lenora, I don't let others take what belongs to me. And *you* belong to me. Every whimper, every tremor, every moment of your pleasure is mine." He nuzzled her neck. "Do not hide from me, little one."

"All... alright," she agreed.

He kissed her in reward, then turned back to his task, moving along her body sinfully. It may have been for her pleasure, but Alistair obviously delighted in his task, tasting her thoroughly.

*If only the people of Mossley knew how that dragon would truly eat me!* They'd have been scandalized.

But it was impossible to think of them for long when Alistair tongued her so thoroughly. He sucked her bud, not hard but insistent, and it made Nora feel like she was approaching something. A cliff, a wave, threatening to slam into her and end her. Her heart beat faster and faster.

"It's too much," she cried.

Still, he continued. If anything, her cries made him more determined, looking up at her from under his lashes.

But this much pleasure, more than she could have ever conceived of, had turned frightening.

"Alistair, I can't! You... you'll end me!"

At this, he stopped. Not abruptly—he instead returned to her core, long licks, teasing as he gently released the pressure that had threatened to overwhelm her. His fingers returned, coaxing at her entrance.

"Tell me, precious one... you say you've known no man, but surely you know your own body."

She looked at him, confusion wading through the fog of bliss he'd crafted around her.

"Haven't you made yourself orgasm before?" he asked.

Nora bit her lip. She had heard the term, in the raunchiest tavern, and wasn't entirely uneducated having seen the barn animals... but she had never applied such things to herself.

Alistair would not take mercy on her until she answered, the relentless creature. So reluctantly she shook her head, still meeting his gaze because he would surely redirect her if she looked away.

It was a hard task, especially while his fingers still moved in her, teasing, tempting.

His expression turned contemplative, but it was not an unkind look. He looked at her like she was the most delicate puzzle he had ever seen. It made Nora feel almost safe in her confession, however fraught it had been.

"Humans can be so primitive..." he muttered. "It's a crime for you to have been denied so long. I should make you come right now, on my tongue."

She opened her mouth to protest, but Alistair wasn't done.

"But as I said, I'm a greedy dragon. And while I have no doubt I would enjoy that, I'm selfish enough that I want your first time to be with your wet, hungry hole filled with my cock. Where I can look into your eyes as the pleasure overtakes you."

His words sent a jolt directly down to her core, as potent as his mouth had been.

"Do you like that, Lenora? Do you like the idea of coming on my cock?"

When she didn't answer, his fingers stilled. They didn't leave her, but rather paused exactly where they were.

In a way that made her even more aware of their position. Of what they might be replaced by. Of how that might feel. Of how her hips moved even now, trying to urge them back to motion.

She nodded.

"Use your words, precious one. I want to hear your tongue tell me your every filthy desire," he coaxed.

She swallowed. "I want... I want to feel you inside me."

"And?" he urged, his eyes hungry.

"I want you to..." What was the word he used? "To make me come."

A bright grin exploded across Alistair's face. It nearly froze Lenora on the spot. He was so lovely, so tender in that moment, that it seemed impossible to believe she had ever feared him.

"Then I shall do just that," he vowed. "But first, I must ready you."

"How much more ready could I be?" she whimpered as his fingers resumed their ministrations. His other hand favored her breast, tugging and toying.

"My brave, impatient human," he murmured, dotting her jaw with kisses. "Your mind may be ready, but if I'm to not hurt you, your body must be as well."

She wanted to argue—now that he'd planted the seed, it seemed hardly fair to make her wait—but he silenced her with a kiss. And while his tongue entered her mouth, a third finger went to her core.

She bucked at the invasion, and his cock jolted back, the hard length pressing on her thigh.

A potent reminder to be patient.

Finally, when she thought she would nearly drown in pleasure anew, he deemed her ready. His fingers withdrew, and she almost sobbed at the loss.

But just as quickly as they withdrew, his length pressed against her, the head of his cock teasing at the entrance.

"Don't make me wait any longer," she begged. She barely recognized her voice.

Alistair loosed a groan, letting the first part into her body. "Don't say things like that, precious one. You could make a centuries-old dragon forget himself."

He was large. He was so large she wondered if she might have made a mistake, a grave miscalculation, because it was entirely possible dragons and women were not meant to fit as such.

But still, she wanted him.

He continued to coax her body, teasing with his mouth and fingers, rubbing her bud so she might spread her legs, letting his hips dip lower between her as he eased in.

It was scary.

Yet if she thought herself frightened, Alistair seemed nigh tortured as he moved at a glacial pace, constantly searching her face for signs of pain.

It was not exactly comfortable. Being bludgeoned seldom was. But it was not the pain that she'd heard the other girls in the village describe.

"It's okay," she assured him. How strange, yet how right the words felt. "I can take it."

Alistair's gaze held her while he finally sank the rest of the way.

And then, just as he'd sheathed himself, he began to move back. She nearly protested, but he didn't go far. He thrust back in a short distance, then farther back and faster, building a tempo.

Nora had never felt anything like it. Never felt so full, so pleasured, so connected with another being. His breaths drew quicker and Nora found that was a type of pleasure too, to see the effect she had on the great obsidian dragon that had terrorized their country for years.

The powerful, immortal creature—and it found pleasure in her. He pushed deeper into her, faster and more forceful than before. She gasped.

"Was it too much?" he asked, frozen above her.

She lifted her hips in answer. "More, Alistair, more."

"I should be gentle." The words were as much to himself as to her, as if he could ward off his darker nature.

"Be as you are," she demanded, pulling him down for a kiss. "I may be weaker than you, but I am not made of glass."

"Weak is the last term I would use to describe the woman who tried to murder me," he teased.

Before she could apologize again, he obeyed her, thrusting deeper, faster. He no longer asked questions of her body, but demanded. Demanded she take him fully, that she moan and gasp and not stifle a sound, that she give everything to him.

Nora was helpless to obey.

It was the most wonderful kind of helpless.

Her pleasure grew and grew. It was different this time, less terrifying than when he'd licked her. And more equal, because while she edged closer and closer, so too did her dragon lover. His grunts and groans sent thrills down her spine, made her wrap her legs around his sculpted hips as if to stop him from leaving.

"Do you feel it?" he asked. "Your orgasm building?"

She nodded frantically. It was there, it was so close.

"I as well." He barely got the words out. "I want you to come when I do, Lenora Tashe. Want to feel you contract around me while I spend my seed."

She didn't know how to obey, how to withstand him, but her body knew. He plunged into her over and over, pleasure growing like a wildfire inside her, about to consume the very last drop of her restraint.

"Now," he commanded.

She exploded. Her pleasure crested over that final hill, ecstasy sparking in her body. She had wanted to see the moment of her dragon's spend, but it was impossible to do more than close her eyes while it rolled over her.

Never. Never had she known. Time lost meaning. All she knew was she was in heaven, warm, protected, full.

# Chapter 10

ALISTAIR OBSIDIAN-CLAW HAD NEVER come so hard in his entire immortal life. His twin flame was indeed a fiery thing. Not only had she taken everything he had given her, she had demanded more. Despite her initial hesitation, she had trusted him to guide her to pleasure.

Now, she curled up atop his chest, her breaths coming slow and even as she drifted off to sleep in his arms.

Alistair should have felt restless—a dragon never slept well away from the seat of its hoard, and his golden mountain had been the only place he'd found solace since he'd first amassed it. He had no desire to wake his mate by carrying her over there. She had earned a rest after the day she'd had.

It was more than sexual satiation that eased his ever-tense muscles. There was a blood-deep contentment that settled him for perhaps the first time in his life.

*My mate. Mine.*

She was a more precious gift than he ever imagined.

Woe be to anyone who dared try to take what was his...

Despite the dark, he studied her with perfect vision. The flush that remained across her skin, fading slowly. The curve of her ear, peeking out from tendrils of yellow hair. The feeling of her little nails as they curved against his chest, the nails clear and pink, unlike his obsidian ones.

The scars.

Even now, the sight threatened to send him into a rage. He decided to view them differently. Were they evidence someone had dared abuse his Lenora? Yes. But they were also proof that his mate was strong. She was not one to shatter, to whimper. She was one to attempt to murder the dragon who had taken her (as was his due) in his sleep; some violence from another human would not break her.

Still, the person who did it would die. It was simply a matter of coaxing the name she was so reluctant to give from her lips. He admired her loyalty, but it was misdirected. In time, it would belong to him alone. She *would* confide in him, and he then would destroy whoever had done this.

But he was a dragon. He had time.

And if not, well, he could simply set the entire continent ablaze. That ought to take care of the problem just as well, though his mate might disapprove.

He expected her to sleep the rest of the night, but the female roused in his arms only a smattering of hours later.

For a moment, she startled, as if having forgotten where she was. He settled her back, stroking her exposed skin with a tenderness he hadn't known himself capable of.

"So this wasn't a dream," she murmured.

He grinned. "If this is typical for your dreams, then I should very much like to visit them, precious one."

She chuckled against him. It was the first genuine laugh he had heard from her. The sound sent a bolt of arousal down to his member, causing him to stiffen.

She felt it, too. "Surely you couldn't want more after that."

The poor thing sounded scandalized, so he hid his grin. "Lenora Tashe, I'll always want more of you." It would sound like banal flattery to her mortal ears, instead of the simple truth it was. He could go a dozen more times that evening if she wished, but he had no salve ready for any bruises she might gain from his rough lovemaking. Such items hadn't warranted a place in his hoard before; he would have to rectify that. Perhaps take a stray healer in to create a vat.

"You can call me Nora, you know. Everyone else does. Or did, I guess." She didn't sound overly upset at the correction, he noted. Perhaps it would be easier to coax the name of the offender than Alistair expected.

"Do you dislike when I call you by your name?"

She considered, then shook her head, blonde tresses caressing his bare chest. "I suppose not. It's just that no one else does."

"Mmm. That pleases me. I like having your name all to myself."

She snorted. "You really are greedy about strange things."

"I'm a dragon."

"And that explains it all, doesn't it?"

As far as Alistair was concerned, it did. He was a dragon. And she was his twin flame.

He would have to tell her that.

Not tonight. Not while she was still wary. Soon, though.

"Tell me, Lenora"—he found he truly did enjoy saying her name all the more now that it was *his*, as far as he was concerned—"what were you attempting to do, stabbing me with my own scale?"

She froze in his arms like startled prey, and Alistair exhaled in frustration. "I'm not upset, as I told you. I'm simply curious. The only thing that could upset me is if you attempted to flee again, and you won't, correct?"

She eased back, twisting slightly so she might look at him. Since he had let the flames on the walls go out for her to sleep, it was impossible for her feeble human eyes to see him as he did her. With a thought, he stirred the lights again. He wanted her to look at him. He wanted her to be as obsessed with him as he was with her.

"I barely think I could stand at this moment, so no, I won't flee," she agreed. "But wouldn't most anyone be angry if someone tried to kill them?"

"Anyone else might be in danger. I am in none; I'm invulnerable." For the moment. Now that he had his Lenora, that would change. But the thought was not as frightening as he might have expected. Treasure came with a cost—you had to protect it. The most valuable prize of all was surely worth a genuine threat of death.

Lenora blew a breath through her mouth.

"Displeased?" Alistair teased. Or maybe it was not a jest; maybe she really wanted him dead. He would fix that, if it were true. Though it might be a bit of a blow to his ego.

"No, no. It's just... I was told by that old woman, the same one who convinced the village to offer me up, that a dragon only lowers its guard in its hoard and sheds its scales and that those scales can pierce it..." She trailed off, considering him anew.

His clever mate. He grinned. "You're thinking perhaps the shedding was less literal, and that a discarded obsidian scale could pierce my heart while I am in this form. That would be incorrect. I am as indestructible in this shape as when I wear my wings."

"I guess it was nonsense then. Along with the rest."

"The rest?"

A fresh blush colored her cheeks. "She also said I was to wed you, and that would save the village."

Perhaps there was more to this seer than any in the village realized. Especially if she had correctly foreseen what Lenora was to him. It was likely the rest of what she had said was correct as well, but the words had been miscast. His own self did not refer to his scales, but the being that was part of his soul. Because Lenora Tashe was more than his mate.

She was the only female capable of killing him.

## Chapter 11

NORA DIDN'T KNOW WHAT to make of her new life. The changes were nearly innumerable. She slept on a pile of gold, with a dragon wrapped around her—sometimes in his human skin, sometimes in his scales. She had a little beast that followed at her heels throughout the day. She had food she didn't need to fetch herself. Her clothing was as grand as the queen's, if not even finer. She bathed daily in a hot underground pool, and nearly every day she made love in that very pool with the same dragon that had taken her.

But the most stunning one was this: she was happy.

It was especially startling, because Nora had never considered herself someone to be *un*happy. Yet now, with her current mood in stark relief to the past one, she realized that she had merely survived from one desperate day to the next.

With Alistair, she wasn't simply making it from one day to the other. She was enjoying them. He liked to make her laugh; he seemed to set it as a goal. And he succeeded. The dragon could be quite funny when he set his mind to it, and she found she enjoyed teasing him back, enjoyed coaxing the rough sound of his laugh until it no longer sounded so rusty from disuse.

More than simply making her laugh, he was eager to please her. And not just her body. He indulged her mind as well. He told her stories of far-off kingdoms, of lands unlike anything she had ever seen, and of creatures as wondrous as—or slightly less than, as he'd emphasized—dragons. There were more dragons in the world than just him, and he taught her about them, their culture, their values. He even mentioned a brother, another obsidian dragon who had left the too-small kingdom in search of a new land. It was not simply greed that drove them, though he was not ashamed of his base nature. Their wealth, their hoard, was directly tied to their power. The most powerful dragons had one thing incapable of being stolen in their hoards—love. A twin flame, he described, was a soul carved from the same embers as the dragon's.

He had looked at her meaningfully when he told the story. Perhaps letting her know there would always be something else, a way to inform her he had his mind on other treasure. But it hardly mattered, Lenora decided. If he had not found his twin flame by now, he would likely not find it while she was still alive, and she could keep her dragon for herself in the meantime.

When the stories weren't enough, he availed her to the rest of his collection. Where books had been a rare commodity in Mossley, and she'd only been taught letters so she could manage her stepmother's legal documents, Alistair seemed to have an unending supply.

Jealous as he was, he didn't mind when her attention was on books or anything else she explored in the cavern. Sometimes, he bid her to read to him, as he explained he never quite had the patience to go through them himself. Yet he was quite literate, and when she stumbled over words, he helped her along, ever patient.

Alistair especially enjoyed the romantic ones. And sometimes he acted out scenes with her. First in jest, and then in a way that left them both breathless and collapsed on the cave floor.

So yes, Nora was happy. Happier than she had any right to be, she suspected. And the happiness continued until she made a grave mistake.

It was some months after she had come to live with the obsidian dragon. They had just gone for a third round that day and settled into one of the massive beds in the main cavern, Morthil dozing some distance away.

"Isn't this more comfortable than a mountain of metal?" she teased.

"It's not just metal. It's *gold*." He drew out the word as if it was a very important distinction to understand.

It was. But where once she'd been alarmed by the wealth Alistair surrounded himself with, she now had simply accepted it as part of him.

"It's cold and hard," she insisted, just because it was sometimes fun to rile the dragon. Even if she'd come to realize he was not her enemy, not in truth anymore.

"It's actually rather malleable," he groused. "Are you so used to a bed you cannot adapt?"

He indulged her on every front, but he truly did prefer to sleep on that mountain of gold. Of course, more than that, he refused to sleep separately, and Lenora found she liked the warmth of his body surrounding her enough that the gold wasn't so bad, certainly not with the pile of textiles.

She snorted. "I'm not used to beds at all. Can't recall having slept in one before coming here, actually. It's why I'm so keen to try it out."

Alistair frowned slightly. He was propped on his side, one hand carelessly toying with her hair while he spoke with her, their legs in a tangle. "Have human tastes changed so much? I thought beds were common for your kind."

"They are. I just never had one."

"Why?"

Nora wasn't sure what it was. Maybe it was the fact she was truly happy for the first time in her life and no longer felt the need to constantly remind herself that she should be grateful for everything her stepmother had done for her. Maybe it was the way Alistair never seemed to judge her harshly or insult her—at least not outside of odd comments about her lack of appreciation for sleeping on piles of gold. Maybe they had simply spent enough time together.

"We only had one bed in the cottage, my stepmother's." There had been two, but hers had been moved to make way for her stepmother's belongings. "Hers was large enough to share, especially since my father died shortly after they married, but she said I took up too much space, and that the hearth was a more comfortable spot. So I didn't have a bed."

"Did you not have money for one?"

"No, we weren't destitute. My stepmother, Helga, didn't see the point in getting a second bed. She felt the ground was more than enough, and especially since my chores included tending to the livestock, there was no sense in letting me get animal filth onto clean sheets that would then need to be laundered. Even though she had me launder her sheets every few days." She snorted. "Though with all the cinders around the fireplace, I daresay I was usually dirtier than the animals. She insisted good care be taken of them, and if she ever found my care lacking, if I was a half hour late getting the feed in the morning, or too slow to finish milking the cattle... she let me know of her displeasure. And how lucky I was that she cared for me, even though my father was no longer alive."

"Did she do this to you?" He fingered her back. The scars no longer pained her, not after Alistair had taken to applying some poultice he'd gotten after her first week and kept in regular supply since.

"Yes. It was her. It wasn't often, maybe every other season or so. It was just... after my father died, I was unruly. She said it helped her 'guide me.'"

The change over Alistair was subtle, but instant. His reptilian eyes narrowed, the pupils thinning to slits. He blinked as if to cast it away, but Lenora had not missed it.

And even though Alistair did not immediately bolt from the bed, did not so much as frown, let alone curse the woman the way Nora sometimes did, she knew she had made a very bad mistake.

## Chapter 12

ALISTAIR SPENT THE NIGHT plotting while Lenora slept in his arms. For once, he did not move her from the four-poster bed she adored, even though it was not as good as the mountain of gold he'd amassed.

His female had admitted the avalanche of textiles he'd put atop made it comfortable, but she still seemed to enjoy the cachet a bed represented. He resolved that the next night he would simply move the bed atop the pile, solving both issues.

He was in quite a problem-solving mood. Though his thoughts were far from sleeping arrangements.

The stepmother.

At last, she had offered him the missing piece of the puzzle. And now he could mete out justice against those who had dared harm his mate.

When he had first learned she had been abused, he had fought the urge to go turn the entire worthless village of Mossley to ashes. In his view, they were all complicit in her mistreatment. But there were two issues with such a thing. One, the person directly responsible might not suffer enough—unacceptable. And two, there might be people Lenora had cared about there. Friends perhaps, though she'd made no mention of them. Parents were another possibility. She might take issue with him killing them in his quest for justice.

Any imagined parents were absolutely worthless in his view for allowing their daughter to be so mistreated, but his sensitive Lenora would feel differently. So he had resisted his initial urge to simply go set the entire village ablaze.

But now he had a name.

Night twisted back to day, and his Lenora roused, looking lovely as ever. She rubbed the sleep from her eyes and grinned at him.

"See? Isn't a bed restful?" She flashed a brilliant smile at him. It was almost enough to make Alistair postpone his plans so he could spend the day in bed with her, worshiping her body.

Instead, he agreed, ignoring the fact he himself hadn't bothered to sleep—it was a pastime he enjoyed but did not require. He did insist she stay in bed while he fixed a hearty breakfast for her. In their months together, he'd come to learn several of her preferences. He'd also helped her discover ones she hadn't had the opportunity to explore before. This morning, her breakfast included a half-pound of dragon fire-grilled sausage and bacon, fresh bread, strawberry preserves, dry-aged cheese, accompanied by several sweet confections he'd procured that solicited the most wonderful sounds from Lenora when she had first sampled them.

Naturally, it was all served on golden trays. And naturally, she shared half of it with Morthil who had been resting on the ground beside the bed and since usurped his spot where Lenora now stroked his ears. The swallump purred at her ministrations, and Alistair hand-fed her since her hands were now busy.

And just because he enjoyed it.

"I was thinking I might start categorizing all your books today," she told him between bites. "I've read so many now it's hard to keep track."

He bent down to lick a stray bit of jam from the corner of her lips. "That sounds very nice, precious one. I'll be gone on an errand today, but I'll be back by nightfall. Morthil will guard you."

"An errand? Where?"

"Your old village, Mossley. The time to tithe has come."

She jerked back, aghast. "It hasn't been a year yet!"

He gave a careless shrug, standing from his perch at the bedside. "I'm a dragon. I'm entitled to my whims."

"But... but they won't be able to pay."

"Oh, I don't think that will be an issue."

"Well, I do," she argued. "Let me come with you."

Alistair considered for a moment. He hadn't wished to upset her with the horrors he was about to inflict, but maybe it was just as well. Once Lenora saw how well he could defend her from any who would harm him, she would surely be willing to accept the twin flame bond. For he still had not told her about it entirely, unsure she would accept.

They were in the air a scant half hour later. Instead of in his claws, she rode atop him. They had gone out on adventures in the months since, and he was pleased with how she had come to love the air, come to trust that he would keep her safe.

"Why are you really going?" she called from atop his back. "Why Mossley?"

"Because that is where the scum who dared disfigure you lives."

"You can't mean to kill my stepmother! How is that a tithe?"

"Did she not offer you up to me, the first of that ignorant mass to decide you were a fair sacrifice? Trying to save her own life in exchange for yours?" It may have been the best thing to ever happen to Alistair, but his mate had been frightened all the same. So, he felt no gratitude there.

"That was different," Lenora argued. "The entire village thought it was in their best interests. They thought it would end the tithing."

"Then I shall offer them a deal. If the village agrees to give me your stepmother, I will never require them to tithe again. And this time, they will not have to bank on the words of a seer who does not speak for me."

Lenora was silent for a long moment, obviously trying to find some hole to poke in Alistair's argument. But it was a fair deal. It was also one he offered because he had no doubt they would agree. For if they were willing to relinquish Lenora, they must be willing to do anything.

They landed in Mossley while the sun was high in the sky. There was, as to be expected, a great deal of screaming, fleeing, more screaming, and an unpleasant, but not altogether unexpected, amount of urination.

But none were willing to take up a weapon. Obviously, it would be futile, as they knew.

Yet it hadn't stopped his bride. Yet another way they were unworthy of her.

She was hidden on his back. He could have used her for a mouthpiece, but instead, he deigned to speak to the mortals.

"Bring me the one called Helga Tashe. If you give her to me, I will never again seek a tithe from Mossley."

Silence.

Then the screaming resumed. Alistair didn't concern himself with following the conversations that immediately followed, the debates, the searches, and so on. Less than an hour later, a stringy, red-faced woman was brought in front of him. Her hands were bound, and a cloth gag was around her mouth.

"Is this her?"

Thinking the words were for them, the village leadership fell over themselves assuring him that they would never dare attempt to deceive the great and powerful dragon. But he only listened for Lenora's confirmation, which came quietly from behind his neck.

Finally. He'd devised any number of ways to torture the woman into regret, but now that she was in front of him, he nearly lost control of his anger. He inhaled, preparing to incinerate the witch.

"Wait!"

# Chapter 13

THERE WERE GASPS AT the sound of her voice, loud enough to be heard even from the height of a dragon.

Revealed, Lenora stood, looking out from behind Alistair's massive neck. In front of them, despite the initial terror, a gathering had drawn together. Nora had listened, nearly sick to her stomach, while they made the easy decision to sacrifice her stepmother.

It wasn't that she had affection for her stepmother. No, the past few months had put it all in a new light. But it hurt, all the same, to hear how little the people of Mossley cared about each other.

"You can't do it here!" she insisted.

"And why not?" Alistair did not sound pleased to be interrupted, but at least he had listened to her.

"Because you'll burn the village too," she said.

She wondered if she should've had some stronger reason. Should've argued for Helga's life, after how she'd spent years raising Nora. Yes, she'd been cruel at times, but she hadn't forced Nora to sleep out in the cold... not often anyway.

But she couldn't bring herself to speak any words in her stepmother's defense.

"Very well. I will take this hag some distance and deal with her. In the meanwhile, you will stay here among the villagers until I return."

He adjusted so Nora could dismount.

"No harm shall come to Lenora Tashe while I deal with your latest gift." Alistair's words did not come as a roar, but it made no difference. Everyone heard the threat of violence in them.

And then he was gone, the gagged protests of her stepmother lost to the wind.

Nora braced for censure after how she was complicit in Alistair's demands, but it did not come.

"Nora's alive!" Friar Jeffreys exclaimed.

"She convinced the dragon to spare the village," a young woman joined in.

"And to end the tithe, just as Bess had said," another added. This was the mayor.

Slowly they edged closer. Not too close, though. She realized why. She may have been one of them once, but no longer. She was part of a dragon's hoard, not a person.

Even if she had killed him, it was unlikely they would have revered her. If anything, she would have come back and been placed back under her stepmother's thumb.

The first to truly approach her was none other than Crazy Bess. The nickname was a bit cruel, but then, so was convincing the town to give her up for the tithe. "So, you visit us at last."

"It's not like he listens to me," Nora grumbled.

"That's not what it looks like."

Okay, Alistair did listen to Nora, to a point. He'd let her come and halted his flame when she'd told him to. But he was still a capricious creature, and it was unlikely she would ever tame him.

But Nora didn't feel obliged to agree aloud. "That stuff you told me about how to kill a dragon didn't work at all. I stabbed Ali—the dragon," she corrected, not wanting to give up his name, "with his own scale my first night there and it didn't so much as tickle him."

Bess laughed, the creaking sound drawing worried glances from the denizens of Mossley who were nearest.

"My prophecy was quite exact," Bess countered. "You simply misunderstood. By sending you to the tithe, the dragon has now agreed to stop requiring anything further from us, keeping our village safe. And that only occurred because he has let his guard down and listened to your counsel."

"But you couldn't have known that would happen," Nora argued.

Bess just raised an uneven brow, as if to reply, *Couldn't I?*

"And the stuff about me being able to pierce his heart?"

But Bess's answer was drowned out by the returning flap of wings.

A gangly figure pushed forward, even as the wind roared with Alistair's approach. "Nora, wait!"

It was Garth, the farmer's son, who had escorted her to the tithe. The one she had considered tumbling with a summer ago.

"We're going," Alistair growled. Clearly disliking Garth's approach, he didn't wait for Nora to mount, instead encircling her with his claws without so much as landing.

Garth didn't back away. "We thought you were dead, if we'd known... it's one thing to be eaten but another to be his victim," he stammered as Alistair began to take flight. "I'll make this right, Nora! I promise!"

His foolish calls spurred Alistair higher. Knowing how much the dragon disliked people encroaching on his hoard, she admired his restraint.

Garth was still yelling foolish vows.

"I don't need saving!" she called back.

But it was lost to the wind.

They flew back to Alistair's mountain, or home, as Nora found herself thinking of it, that same day.

She was surprised by the relief that she felt returning to the now familiar cave.

"Are you unhappy with me?" Alistair tossed the words out carelessly, nonchalantly as he slid his now-human legs into skin-tight leather trousers.

Nora had been too busy admiring the view to track his thoughts. "Come again?"

"For what I did to your stepmother."

Nora didn't know the details of what Alistair had done, nor was she curious. But there was no doubt the woman was now dead, and it was unlikely there were any bones left to bury.

She should have been troubled. Even on the flight over, she had felt a growing anxiety because she should be upset, should be defending the woman who had raised her, but in her true heart, she could not find so much of a scrap of affection or kindness for the woman who had cruelly beaten and abused Nora since she was a child.

That realization had distressed her more than the actual prospect of her stepmother dying. That she might be so callous. It made her want to lie to Alistair about her true feelings, to rail at him that he had committed a terrible act of villainy she wouldn't forgive, but it would be hollow. And he had never been less than honest with her.

"No. I'm not. I should be, but we weren't close, and it's as you said. The village decided."

After living with Alistair, seeing how he cared for her even though she was nothing more than a piece of his hoard, how he despised the thought of anyone lifting a hand against her, no, she couldn't bring herself to feel a single drop of remorse for what Alistair had done. Nora had been a child under her care. She hadn't deserved the cruel treatment then. And she certainly hadn't deserved to be given up to a villainous dragon—no matter how caring the dragon had turned out to be.

Alistair shepherded her deeper into the caves. Though she now knew them well enough not to stumble even in the dark, she enjoyed the opportunity to cling to him. Sometimes she even let him carry her.

"I just wish to understand why it mattered so much to you. Because you disliked the idea of someone touching one of your belongings?"

"It's because I loathed the idea of someone touching *you*." The force behind his words startled her. "I will keep you safe from any who would dare to harm you. And those who have already done so will be punished. This is my vow to you."

"No one else has harmed me," she assured him, her words soothing the protective beast.

"And no one ever will again."

So he took her there, against the tunnel wall where her cries could echo throughout the entire cave. Then again on the four-poster bed which now sat atop the pile of textiles that was already on the mountain of gold.

And when it was late, she dozed off, content in her dragon lover's arms. Something warm settled in her chest, something that felt like more than her own gentle feelings, as though there was another presence twin to her own. It was the most comforting thing she'd ever felt.

Relaxed as she was, she did not bother to rouse herself enough to voice her worries, the way Garth's promises to rescue her still rang in her ears—surely, they meant nothing.

## Chapter 14

ALISTAIR AND NORA SPENT a great deal of time together in the caves. However, they did not spend *all* their time together.

And so, one week after the events at Mossley, Alistair had left to go acquire some provisions. And though Nora offered to join him, her attentive dragon didn't miss the awkward way she walked, still sore from the vigorous activity of last night—and this morning—and so he insisted she stay home to rest.

Nora missed him. It wasn't that she wasn't comfortable on her own. But she found herself lingering by the entrance of the cave all the same, glancing up at the sky every few minutes while she settled to read the latest book he had gotten for her. (Alistair had more books than she could ever hope to read, but she had taken a liking to one author in particular, and he had gone out of his way to hunt down the next book in the series.)

Morthil had remained deep in the caves; the sunlight bothered the creature's sensitive eyes. Nora was alone with her book. For a time.

It was not the sight of wings on the horizon that drew her attention. Instead, it was a noise from below.

Other humans.

"Nora Tashe?" an unfamiliar voice called. "Are you there? We saw the dragon leave."

Curiosity drew her to the edge. And there, she saw the last person she had ever expected.

"You are alive!" The Prince of Wyrdova peered up at her. His steel armor glittered in the daylight, nearly blinding her. "Fear not, fair maiden. We are here to rescue you at last."

Nora had two thoughts in quick succession.

*I'm not a maiden anymore.*

*And I certainly don't wish to be rescued.*

She stammered as much of the latter as she could, but the prince continued unperturbed, accompanied by half a dozen knights. Assured of her presence, they continued to scale the cliffside.

Nora wanted to retreat into the cave. But if she did, they would just follow her deeper and deeper, and should Alistair return and find them with his hoard, he would be utterly enraged. They didn't deserve to die for trying to rescue her.

The prince appeared before her, and against her better judgment, she took a half-step back.

She had seen him only once before, on the day of the tithing.

"Prince, I appreciate you coming all this way—"

"'Twas nothing, fair Nora." He interrupted her with a brilliant flash of white teeth. "That blond boy, Garth from... Moseisely? Mosslo? Well, whichever. He rode all the way to the castle to tell us that you had not, in fact, been eaten by that evil dragon."

So it was Garth she had to thank for this mess.

"On my honor," the prince continued without so much as bothering to breathe. "I could not bear to leave you in his clutches a day longer, so I have traveled with great haste to come and rescue you."

She couldn't help but notice that the prince who had made great haste was clean shaven without a single freshly combed hair out of place. He looked more like he was about to sit for a noble portrait than to rush off, but she shouldn't be so uncharitable. His heart surely had been in the right place.

"Now, let us go," he finished, extending an armored arm in her direction and already twisting his body, expecting her to follow.

At last, he paused long enough for Nora to interject. "I don't need rescuing."

He turned back to her, his perfect smile going sideways for a moment before he recovered. "Ah, you're one of those modern maidens, aren't you, who feel somehow undermined if a nobleman rescues you? Truly, Nora, there is no shame in having a knight come to your aid when you have no hope of escape. Especially if it is a prince like myself." He winked in a way that said that was especially an honor.

Nora was beginning to feel queasy. "I appreciate your efforts, Prince," she said, trying hastily to soothe his ego. "But what I mean to say is I have no plans to escape at all. And not"—she said hastily before he could interrupt—"because I have resigned myself to a miserable existence and cannot conceive of the familiar life that you would return me to. I am happy right where I am. In fact, I am happier here than ever before. I will not deny the dragon has been taxing on the kingdom, but he has not been cruel to me. So, please, it is an honor for you to have taken the time to inquire about my wellbeing, and I hope you have a speedy departure before the dragon returns." *And now leave me alone*, she finished with her eyes.

But the prince did not turn to the exit and depart. Instead, a look of rage came over him.

"You insolent chit," he seethed. "You're coming with me. And that is an order from the royal crown of Wyrdova."

When Nora did not immediately leap to obey, he decided to take her by force. He grabbed her by the arms and swiftly overpowered her, bidding one of the knights to take control of her, which he did, if a bit apologetically.

"Just leave me be!" she demanded, flailing helplessly against his armor.

The prince ignored her.

In short order, they moved back down the mountainside and piled her onto the prince's horse. In a dreadful, ironic way, it was almost a mirror to her trip to the tithing those months ago.

She kept arguing and arguing, even when the prince threatened to gag her. She silenced only when he finally snapped that it seemed the dragon was more dangerous than ever they'd thought if he could use his powers to control the minds of feeble women and turn them against the crown, and they would have to return to hunt the beast down if the control didn't wear off.

A veiled threat—obey, or they'd come back with an army for Alistair. Obviously, the prince had staked his pride on rescuing Nora, and the spoiled brat would settle for nothing less. If she continued to argue, he might well make good on his threat, and despite all of Alistair's assurances no mortal could kill him, she didn't want to see him harmed. So she said no more.

She wished Alistair would rescue her.

It was a silly hope. To Alistair, she was just a *thing*. A thing he liked, a part of his hoard he enjoyed, sure. But just one piece, no more valuable than a hunk of metal. To her, he was so much more. He was the one she thought of when she woke, when she read a witty passage in a book she wanted to share, when Morthil did a particularly charming trick. He was the one who made her chest flutter and ache. But for him, that person was destined to be someone else, some mythical twin flame.

So no, she did not believe Alistair would come for her.

And when she was cowed into silence and the fact settled over her, a choking noose that made it hard to breathe, Nora wept.

## Chapter 15

Alistair watched as Lenora left his cave, escorted by half a dozen human knights.

His first instinct was to swoop in, light them all on fire, and inform his little human exactly what he thought of her attempt to escape.

It was a dragon's instinct, after all. To keep what was part of his hoard.

But that was the trouble. He had come to learn Lenora was not a thing he could own. She was her own person. She was his *equal*. If he wanted her, he had to make her want to stay, to smile at him, to tease him, to laugh with him. And he had tried. He had tried so damn hard these past few months to give her everything he could imagine that might make her like him enough to accept him.

But it had not been enough. When he had left, in search of a new novel she might read curled up in his lap, along with other staples such as confections that made her sigh and cured meats for Morthil, she had taken the opportunity to leave.

It was agony to watch her go. But if she wanted to leave him after all of this, then she would never be his.

She might be his twin flame, but he was nothing to her. The realization was agony. He faltered in the air, for the first time in centuries, as sadness stabbed at his chest.

If she wished to go, he would allow it. Even if it broke him.

And that decision nearly felled him, until a new sensation impaled him.

In the months since he had become in tune with his twin flames's emotions, seldom had they soured. At most, she grew a bit piqued if he prolonged his teasing without letting her fully enjoy herself.

But he recognized it on instinct.

Sorrow. Distress.

And in answer, Alistair grew furious.

*How dare they?*

*How dare they cause his Lenora distress?*

He descended on them in a matter of seconds. The horses startled at his arrival, the knights struggling to control the horses as they reeled. Only the one that held Lenora was steady, a massive war beast that was likely so inbred it didn't even have the instincts to look afraid.

Much like its rider, the prince.

Alistair met Lenora's gaze. Her eyes glistened, tear tracks highlighting her full cheeks. She couldn't even wipe them away with her hands tied together. The anger that rolled off Alistair should have terrified even her, for he knew he was a fearsome creature to behold. But she did not cower. Instead, her stiff shoulders relaxed at his arrival. The sorrow that stabbed in his heart began to ease.

"Stay back, you foul beast! I command you, as Prince of these fair lands," the male atop the stupid war beast called out.

His reptilian gaze slid to the prince's hands, which held Lenora's bound body between them. A blade was in the foolish boy's right hand, primed not to attack Alistair... but to threaten *Lenora*.

The knights fanned out in front of their leader as they regained control of their horses.

A foolish effort.

"You have terrorized this land for far too long, robbing it of its riches. Now, you go too far and take its fine maidens? I tell you, she would rather die than be captured again by you."

The prince was already dead. That had not been in question. But for threatening his Lenora... oh, it would be the hottest flame that eradicated the brat.

Though Alistair was loath to speak to humans—twice in a century (his future bride not included) was too often already—he would not be able to get to her before the prince slashed her throat in a fit of madness with all those knights in his way.

"Very well. If I have taken all your wealth, you may have it back. Send your knights to my cave, and at the heart of the mountain, you shall find my hoard. You can have it all back if you let the woman go."

The prince gripped her tighter, using her body as a shield. *Coward*.

"You lie."

Alistair roared. "Do not question my word, weakling. If all you seek is treasure, then it shall be yours."

Greed lit in the prince's eyes.

"Don't," Lenora pleaded. "It's not worth it. If you lose your hoard—" She cut herself off to stop from revealing secrets, but she knew, as Alistair had told her, his strength was tied to his hoard.

But he would be penniless sooner than he would let someone take his Lenora against her will.

The prince bid his guards to go to the mountain and get all the gold they could carry, but he did not relax his grip on Lenora.

The knights rode away. It was just the three of them now. The prince blustered and blustered. Alistair ignored it, the entire time his gaze fixed on the small female held captive.

The knife gradually loosened as the prince grew tired. It would take the knights time to reach Alistair's mountain.

Minutes ticked by.

And then, when even the birds had quieted, while the three stared at each other in the clearing, a terrifying sound came. A roar so loud, even Alistair nearly flinched.

The prince jerked back in surprise, his horse startling. But Lenora was sharp, and took the chance to jerk her shoulder into the prince, further knocking him off balance. The action made her fall from the horse, her tied hands making it impossible to break her fall.

Alistair caught her in his claws before she ever hit the ground.

And then, because he was altogether furious with the prince, he snapped his neck out and ate him, armor, sword, and all.

## Chapter 16

Alistair placed her on the ground, then shifted from his dragon shape. She flew into his arms, desperate for comfort.

"You—you came," she gasped, tears forming in her eyes.

He wiped the droplets away before they could fall. The sight distressed him. "Of course, dear one. I will always come for you."

She shook in his arms. "I... I wasn't sure," she confessed.

His grip around her tightened. His warmth was a comfort against the fear that had chilled her. The thought of a life without Alistair had been more terrifying than the blade at her throat.

"Let's go before the knights get back," she said. No doubt Alistair could defeat them all, but she didn't want to deal with the confrontation.

"Oh, I'd say there's no chance of that," Alistair assured her.

She tilted her head in question.

"The roar you heard was Morthil. It seems he didn't appreciate the trespassers." A careless what-can-you-do shrug. "Hopefully the indigestion won't be too bad; he's only a juvenile swallump after all. The grown ones can swallow anything without any trouble at all."

"So they were never going to take your treasure? You weren't really going to have to give them anything?" It made sense. His offer had been too dramatic. Naturally, a dragon wouldn't give up his hoard, especially for a human he was affectionate with.

Alistair frowned, his gray eyes narrowing. "Of course, it was a real offer. I didn't know Morthil would do that."

"But if you give up your hoard you'll lose all your strength!"

He cocked a brow at her. "I'm aware."

"You shouldn't do that," she protested. "I'm not worth it. I'm just some peasant you picked up from a village that didn't want to give up any sheep."

"You are worth *everything*."

And with that, he captured her lips. It was a gentle kiss at first, as if he had to reassure himself she was truly in front of him. But she needed more. She needed to feel him against her, to breathe in the smoke on his tongue until it drowned out the fear. She gripped his obsidian black hair and tugged him closer.

When they parted for breath, he nuzzled her cheek. "You are the most important thing in the world to me, Lenora Tashe. Treasure is nothing compared to you. You're not just my heart. You're my twin flame."

She startled back. "What? How?"

"Some things simply are. I've known from the first moment I saw you."

Shock roared through her. All this time she had thought she was nothing more than a passing dalliance for Alistair, because what was one human in the eyes of an immortal dragon?

"Why didn't you say anything?"

"I didn't want to pressure you," Alistair explained, pain in his eyes. "I wanted you to want me for me, not because fate decreed it. When I thought you had chosen to leave, I told myself I should respect your choice." His voice turned soft. "But it was a lie because I could force myself to let you go no more easily than I could carve out my obsidian heart."

"You absolute idiot."

Alistair startled at her language, looking a bit nervous.

"You should have told me," she continued. "Because I love you, and the only reason I didn't tell you is I thought you were destined for another and couldn't see me as anything more than a belonging rather than an equal."

This time, he devoured her lips in a hiss.

"I shall love no other, Lenora Tashe. I could want no other."

And then the mighty dragon did the last thing she ever expected. He sank to his knees before her, gripping the back of her legs with his black-tipped fingers as he gazed up at her with adoration.

"And now I ask, because you are your own person, not my belonging—will you marry me, dear one?"

## Epilogue — Her

Months passed. Although Nora had said yes to Alistair's proposal, they didn't marry right away.

She was impatient to bind herself to the dragon, to claim him as her own, just as he had claimed her, but it was Alistair who delayed.

Oh, he wanted to marry her. He'd assured her of that not just with words but with actions, every night—as well as most mornings and a fair number of afternoons. But he wanted the wedding to be perfect.

"Perfect" to a dragon meant a gown custom-made by the finest tailors in the kingdom, inlaid with precious gemstones, so it glittered like a rainbow. It also weighed almost as much Morthil.

But when the gown was done, and the weather was lovely, Alistair told her it was finally time.

Dragons had no priests; there were no guests except Morthil, who wore a rainbow of sapphires on his collar. He took his shelter under the shade of a tree to avoid the worst of the sun. Concerned, Nora had found an unusual dark bolt of fabric in Alistair's hoard—their hoard, as he insisted it be called—and used it to fashion a veil that blocked any lingering rays.

They'd tried to leave him behind the first time, but Morthil was having none of it. The swallump had bulked up since she had come to live in the cave, likely from the nutritious knights it had swallowed whole. There had, thankfully, been only a limited amount of burping resulting from the large meal.

The wedding did not take place in the cave. Rather, Alistair spirited her off to a hidden valley with a large lake at the center. The sun was high in the sky, making Nora's gown sparkle and reflect on the water as he set her down.

Alistair had explained the ceremony to her several times. A simple exchange of vows, and he would tie his life to hers, sharing his eternal flame.

They would both live a very, very long time.

And as she would now share his flame, she would be the only creature in the world that could render the obsidian dragon vulnerable—as Bess had said, when she wed the beast, she would gain that power over him.

"It's not too late to back out," Alistair whispered in her ear.

He was dressed in finery to match her own. A black silk suit, golden hardware at his buttons and cuffs, a cape draped over his shoulder pinned in place with an enormous diamond.

She gave him a sidelong glance, pretending to fill her gaze with censure when she really just wanted to drink in his appearance. She liked him plenty in tight leather pants and nothing else, but Alistair in formal wear was an *experience*.

"Getting cold feet?" she teased.

"There's not a single part of me that doesn't burn for you, precious one."

His words were playful, but his expression wasn't. He looked at her like she was the most valuable thing in the universe, and he would burn the world to cinders if it pleased her.

He led her to a spot in the clearing and stood across from her, gently lifting her palms atop his own.

"Do you, Lenora Tashe, take me as your twin flame, your eternal partner, the one you shall trust to guard your life above all others?"

"I do. Alistair Obsidian-Claw, do you take me as your twin flame, your eternal partner, the one you shall trust to love your heart above all others?"

He had barely said *I do* before his lips devoured hers.

And they celebrated then and there. Her dragon made quick work of the gown that had taken months to make, jewels soon flying into the lake with a *plink, plink, plink.*

But her dragon didn't care. Because his most valuable treasure was in his arms.

# Epilogue
## Him

AT LAST, SHE WAS his—his twin flame, his fated mate, his *everything*. And he was hers—the dark to her light that would protect her, the mate who would protect her from any who dreamed of harming her.

He had belonged to her for as long as he had existed. But the wedding was a nice touch.

She looked glorious, dressed in the finest jewels, but he could hardly see them. All he saw was *her*.

He would have sworn even her lips tasted different now that she was his wife.

Now, he was eager to know what else tasted different.

He swept her in his arms, eager to rip the dress from her. It may have been a kingdom's—several kingdom's—worth of jewels, but nothing could compare to her naked body. He was hungry for it, now.

"Wait."

He froze over his wife's body. Her breaths were shallow, desire lighting her eyes.

"I... I want to try something. I read about it in a book."

He did love it when she took inspiration from her reading. Loved exploring every part of her sensual nature, helping her discover just what she liked. Looked forward to doing it for as long as the sun burned in the sky. "Then by all means."

She indicated to him to let her down, and he obliged her. He settled against a tree trunk in her direction.

Then she dropped to her knees.

He drew in a thin breath. Flame's take him, he'd never get used to this sight.

"I haven't done this before," she cautioned him. "I'm not sure if you'll like it."

So hesitant. As if there was anything she could do to him that he wouldn't like. He stroked the side of her face, brushing a stray lock from in front of her eyes. *Spun gold.* That was the color of her hair in the sunset light. "Anything you give me, I'll enjoy, precious one. I promise."

She nodded, a small smile as she no doubt heard the sincerity in his words. Then she reached for his trousers and unlaced them. His cock was already hard, his body ready for her.

She lifted her hand to him, holding his obsidian gaze while she pumped the shaft a few times. She might have started as a novice between them, but now, she was an expert with his body. If she wasn't careful, he'd spend right there.

But the stroking stopped, as she gripped his erection and finally lowered her lips to it. She kissed the head, tasting him, then gave an experimental lick with her tongue.

Alistair loosed a groan. Her eyes flicked up and all he could do was rasp, "That's it, love."

She licked him again.

And again.

He threaded his fingers through her hair, not urging her forward but pinning her in place. She grew bolder, taking more of his shaft in her mouth. One hand pumped him, the other sliding over her body which was still covered in that dress.

She was going to end him.

And if so, he would die happy.

She grew bolder as his reactions grew less restrained. He felt his balls tighten, and with restraint he didn't know he had, he gently pulled her away.

"Was it... good?" Nora asked.

"It's *too* good," he explained at her questioning gaze. "I'm not going to spend in your pretty little mouth. Not this first time."

Instead, he slid down to his knees, matching her. With his obsidian claws, he made quick work of the dress, jewels flying everywhere.

Neither of them spared them a second glance.

His mate's breaths were shallow, her chest heaving with excitement. He nuzzled her, unable to stop himself, trailing kisses across her neck, down to her belly. She tasted so good. Like sunshine itself. Every part of her was addictive, perfect.

*And now she was all his.*

His shirt was gone in a heartbeat. Her hands found his chest, tracing the shape of his muscles with her delicate fingertips. He leaned into the touch, his own path continuing down.

Her dress was no match was no match for his supernatural strength. Once the fabric blocked his path, it was gone, jewels flying into the lake.

"Hey!" Nora protested.

His bride's protest was muted as his mouth finally found its destination. Her slit was wet and waiting. He dragged his tongue over the length of her, delighting in her taste and the way she gasped at the contact.

"That's it, precious one. Give me more of that."

Alistair repositioned them so she now sat astride his head while he lay on the grass beneath her. He kneaded her soft flesh between his hands, pinning her against his mouth so he could feast. He licked and teased and tasted until she was panting above him, her moans turning to demands and then to cries as pleasure overtook her. Her thighs contracted around him and he savored the contact. Savored every single part of her as his mouth continued to tend to her while she came.

But he wasn't going to be satisfied with his bride coming only *once*.

Not on his watch.

When she finally returned to him, shifting down his body, her dazed gaze met his. His chest heated with male satisfaction.

"Is it always going to be like this?" she asked softly.

"No." He twisted up to capture her lips. "It's going to get even better."

Her lips curled against his own. "I don't think that's possible."

"Is that a challenge, wife?"

"Maybe."

Well. Alistair *had* always enjoyed a challenge.

"Then let me show you."

She grinned and readied to move off of him, but his hands pinned her in place.

"Not so fast, precious one."

He moved her farther down his body. Through their twin flame bond, he could feel her emotions in her chest as they shifted from confusion to curiosity to blatant interest when she realized what he intended. Another position they hadn't tried before.

His erection curved between her cheeks. Nora pressed her palms against his chest for balance, wide, innocent eyes gleaming wickedly.

"Like this?" she asked.

"I want to see your body move on top of me. Want to feel your tight little hole contracting around me while you ride me, precious one. Taking your pleasure at your own pace."

She lifted her hips, lining herself with his raging cockstand. Then, slowly, carefully, she began to lower herself onto him.

It took all his restraint not to rush her, but he'd never do that. Let her torture him all he liked, as long as she was comfortable.

Finally, he was fully sheathed in her body. She moved experimentally back and forth, feeling his length inside of her.

They fit perfectly.

"Ride me," he groaned.

So Nora began to move. Slow, at first, a shallow lift and dip. Then more while she leaned forward over his body. By the flame, she was lovely. Naked, long strands of hair trailed around her shoulders while her curves moved with her body. Alistair couldn't help but touch her now. He ached to feel every inch of her, to mark her body as his.

Her eyes shut with bliss as she focused on her own pleasure. He could feel her emotions—feel how the sensation overtook her. *Good.* There was nothing more satisfying than seeing his mate claim her own desires. Nothing more satisfying than being the source of it.

"That's it, precious one. Take what you need," he growled.

She moaned, clenching around him. She'd come once, but his bride could do more than that. He'd see to it—and soon, by the way her breaths sped up. "You. Just you."

His own body responded to her words. Close. He was so godsdamned close to the edge.

*Hold on. Have to hold on for her.*

"And you'll have me. For eternity. Now come, precious one. Let me feel you milk me."

Her cheeks flushed even as the rest of her body reacted. He loved the heat on her cheeks. Especially the way he could bring it on with dirty talk after all this time.

His words sent her over, her body spasming as she fell into the grips of another orgasm. He was helpless not to follow her. He came harder than he ever had before, crying out her name.

When the pleasure gave way to exhaustion, she dropped against his body, curling against his chest even as he was still inside her. He brushed a strand of hair from her cheek, curling it around her fingers while his mate panted softly against his chest.

"You sure it's possible to get better than that?" she asked.

"Oh, love," he purred. "You have no idea."

# Acknowledgments

WRITING THIS BOOK WAS probably the most fun I've had writing something... ever. *To Wed an Obsidian Villain* was born in between the second and third book of the Shifted Fates series which, if you've read, I think you'll understand was a heavy story at that point. In contrast, Nora and Alistair's story came from the idea of "What if I just wrote about a man who was absolutely obsessed with spoiling his woman?"

I feel like, as people, but especially as women, wanting things is so often seen as "bad." It's selfish and shameful and lazy to want everything to be taken care of for you. It's too high-maintenance to want a man to give you little gifts, et cetera, et cetera. We're supposed to be completely independent, and maybe you lean on people if in deep trouble, but it's not something we're *supposed* to do. We're supposed to suck it up and solider on. Obviously this is a bit of a sweeping generalization, but it's certainly something I've struggled with unlearning over the years and was struggling with especially at the time I wrote this while I was burning out from my corporate job.

Thank God for fantasy romance, is really all I can say.

So, I hope this book was as fun for you to read as it was for me to write. That said, this book would absolutely have never come to be if I hadn't gotten the opportunity to team up with an amazing group of authors and work on this project. It's been absolutely incredible to get to work with you guys, read your work, combine our efforts to reach hundreds of new readers, and have people to talk to on this often exhilarating (but at times discouraging) journey. So, thank you to Alex, Angelica, Callie, Elayna, Fleur, Jen, Isabella, River, and Sirena. I'm so grateful to have had the chance to work with you and bring all our dragon shifters into the world.

Of course, a special thank you to the incredible Ophelia Wells Langley for ~~herding cats~~ spearheading this project and bringing us together.

Another thank you to the muse behind Morthil, Jenny. I hope your tenacity in begging for deli meats and general hospitality towards visitors was suitably immortalized.

A massive thank you to the team of ARC readers who read Alistair and Nora's story early and shared your love for them. You guys make a huge difference for indie authors like us in getting the word out on new books.

And last, but certainly not least, thank you to you, reader, for coming on this journey. I hope to see you on the next one!

Vasilisa Drake is based in New England and is constantly bouncing from city to city while she tries to find her home amidst overpriced rental apartments. Forsaken Mate was Vasilisa Drake's debut, though she's written contemporary romance under another name for several years. Fantasy romance is her first love, closely followed by pet dragons and men who are obsessed with their women. She can be found staying up way too late reading, organizing her bookshelf for the millionth time, and winning the imaginary arguments in her head at least 30% of the time. You can find her on TikTok and Instagram @VasilisaDrakeBooks or in your inbox if you sign up for her newsletter.

**Want more dragon shifters?**

Be sure to check out the entire Bound by Flame Novella Series.

### Bound by Flame

To Keep an Emerald Rose - Elayna R. Gallea

To Ignite a Pyrite Spirit - Callie Pey

To Snatch a Gilded Laurel - Alex Callan, Angelica Babineaux

To Spare an Opal Soul - River Bennet

To Scorch a Quartz Throne - Fleur DeVillainy

To Hunt a Ruby Remedy - Jen Lynning

To Wed an Obsidian Villain - Vasilisa Drake

To Claim a Silver Curse - Isabella Khalidi

To Embrace an Onyx Heart - Sirena Knighton

## TO WED AN OBSIDIAN VILLAIN

# Find Me

You can find Vasilisa on several platforms including:

Bookbub

Goodreads

Instagram

Romance.io

Storygraph

TikTok

Made in United States
Troutdale, OR
06/23/2024